I AM THE WEAPON

I AM THE WEAPON

THE UNKNOWN ASSASSIN
BOOK 1

ALLEN ZADOFF

LITTLE, BROWN AND COMPANY

NEW YORK   BOSTON

Copyright © 2013 by Allen Zadoff
Excerpt from *I Am the Mission* copyright © 2014 by Allen Zadoff

Little, Brown and Company

Hachette Book Group
1290 Avenue of the Americas, New York, NY 10104
Visit our website at lb-teens.com

Little, Brown and Company is a division of Hachette Book Group, Inc.
The Little, Brown name and logo are trademarks of Hachette Book Group, Inc.

The publisher is not responsible for websites (or their content) that are not owned by the publisher.

First Paperback Edition: May 2014
Originally published in hardcover in June 2013 by Little, Brown and Company as *Boy Nobody*

Library of Congress Cataloging-in-Publication Data

Zadoff, Allen.
  I Am the Weapon / a novel by Allen Zadoff.—1st ed.
    p. cm.
  Summary: Sixteen-year-old Boy Nobody, an assassin controlled by a shadowy government organization, The Program, considers sabotaging his latest mission because his target reminds him of the normal life he craves.
  ISBN 978-0-316-19968-1 (hc) / ISBN 978-0-316-19967-4 (pb)
  [1. Assassins—Fiction. 2. Conduct of life—Fiction. 3. Interpersonal relations—Fiction.
4. High schools—Fiction. 5. Schools—Fiction.] I. Title.
  PZ7.Z21Boy 2013
  [Fic]—dc23
2012029484

10 9 8 7 6

LSC-C

Printed in the United States of America

I AM THE WEAPON

I PICK UP A BASEBALL BAT.

It's a thirty-two-ounce Rawlings composite. I feel the weight in my hands. The balance is slightly off from a dent on the tip.

I grasp the bat on either end and stretch out in the parking lot after the game. Natick vs. Wellesley. My Natick teammates are all around me, high school jocks doing what they do after a win. Celebrating. Big-time.

I celebrate, just like them.

This is what I think to myself:

I am one of you. I am young. I am a winner.

I smile and stretch.

After a moment, I shift my weight onto my back leg and I swing hard. Jack Wu comes up behind me at the same time. The bat misses his head by an inch.

A big man in a black suit tenses nearby. Tenses but doesn't interfere.

This is Jack's bodyguard and driver, a shadow behind Jack whenever he goes out. Jack's dad is rich. Rich and nervous.

Jack hates the bodyguard. He's told me a dozen times. Jack and I are friends, so he tells me these things.

"Watch it with the bat, dude," Jack says, and he punches me on the shoulder. A playful punch.

The Suit steps forward, and Jack spins around, anticipating him.

"Down, Rover," he says, like he's talking to a pit bull.

The Suit grins like he's in on the joke, but I wonder if he wouldn't slap the hell out of Jack if he had the chance. Instead he leans back against the sleek black Mercedes and waits.

"You killed it out there," Jack says. He head-gestures toward the field.

"I do my best," I say.

"Your best kicks ass and takes names," Jack says, and he punches my shoulder again.

This time the big man doesn't move. But the other players are looking at us.

Two punches on the arm. A way of asserting dominance.

Dominance is a threat. It must be dealt with.

I run a checklist in my mind:

I can let him punch me. Choose a lower status.

I can retaliate in equal measure, with equal force.

I can escalate. Assert my dominance.

Which should I choose?

Jack is supposed to be my friend. A teenage friend would punch a buddy the way he punched me. When in doubt, emulate. That's what I've been taught.

So it's option two.

I give Jack a light punch on the shoulder.

"Ow!" he cries in mock pain. "Take it easy on me."

This entire transaction takes no more than two seconds:

I swing the bat.

Jack punches. I punch back.

We both laugh as the Suit looks on.

This is what you'd see if you were watching us now. Two jocks, buddies, teasing each other.

"You want to come back to the bank vault?" Jack says.

The bank vault. That's what Jack calls his house.

"For a little bit," I say.

Jack steps toward the car. The Suit reacts quickly, opening the back door for him.

"My friend is coming with," Jack says to him.

"Yes, sir," he says, and he gestures for me to get into the car.

THE LEATHER IS SOFT IN THE MERCEDES.

It's the kind of leather seat that pulls you in, begs you to relax against it. A seat that says, *You are being taken care of. You are being driven where you need to go.*

I imagine having a father who can afford things like this. Expensive cars. Expensive bodyguards. Not just afford them, but a father who wants his son to have them. Wants him to be taken care of.

But this is not something I should be thinking about now. Not when there's work to do.

I glance at Jack. He's leaning back with his eyes closed.

"I was thinking," he says.

"That's unusual for you," I say.

"Asshole," he says.

He smiles, his eyes still closed.

"I was thinking about you and me."

"Stop right there," I say. "You're making me nervous."

4

"Can I be serious for a minute?" Jack says.

"You want to get all heavy for sixty seconds, I'm not going to stop you."

"I was thinking that you're a real friend."

"You've got tons of friends," I say.

"Not guys I invite over to the house. Not guys I trust."

"You trust me?"

"For real," Jack says.

The Suit in the front seat coughs. A warning to Jack? A reminder that he's still here? Or nothing at all. A tickle in the throat.

"If you trust me, can I borrow a hundred bucks?" I say.

"I don't trust you that much," Jack says.

He laughs.

He punches my arm.

I let him do it.

THE SUIT TYPES A CODE INTO THE SECURITY GATE.

The large metal gate slides open to reveal a long driveway, a guard hut set twenty feet in.

We pull up to the hut and the Suit nods to a guard. He lifts two fingers. Two people coming in, Jack and me. The guard marks it down on a clipboard. He's seen me before, and it's not a big deal.

We continue around a hairpin turn, and the house comes into view. Big but not lavish. The Suit stops to let us out.

Jack types a code to gain access to the house.

The front door beeps to announce our entry. *Front door open*, it says.

It beeps again when the door is closed. *Front door closed*, the electronic voice says.

Jack's dad wanders by with a beer in his hand. Chen Wu is his name. His friends call him John. He's the CEO of a high-tech firm along Route 128. Lots of government contracts.

Does he need all this security?

I know he likes it. It makes you feel important to have a lot of people with guns around you. It makes you feel safe, and more importantly for him, it makes his wife feel safe. That keeps her from giving him a hard time.

It's not just Mr. Wu. All the CEOs are edgy right now. There was some violence a year ago. An important kid got shot during an attempted kidnapping while on spring break in Mexico. The Fortune 500 went security crazy. Now rich kids like Jack need a commando team to take a dump.

"Nice to see you, boys," Jack's dad says.

"What's up, Dad?" Jack says. "Gotta take a squirt. Pardon my French."

He turns to leave.

"Hey, I can't stay too long," I say.

"You gotta go?" Jack says, disappointed.

"Gotta call my mom," I say. "I guess it's morning wherever she is."

"Crap in a bag," Jack says.

He shoots up the stairs.

"You have time for a cold one?" Jack's dad says.

"Beer or soda?"

"How old are you?" he says.

"Sixteen."

"Soda for you. But it was a nice try."

I shrug like I'm bummed out, and I follow him through the den.

"How was the game?" Jack's dad says.

"Amazing," I say. "You should come sometime."

"High school ball is not really my thing," he says.

But it's his son's thing, so what does it matter?

I see this a lot with the Fortune 500. Mr. Wu is always working. Except Friday nights. His only downtime, and he doesn't want to spend it with his family. He relaxes for the evening, then works again all weekend.

So be it. It's Friday night and he's here. So am I.

That's the important thing.

We head into the kitchen, and the conversation drifts to the Red Sox. We're near Boston, so we have to talk Sox.

I notice an expensive knife block on the counter with one of the knives missing from its slot. A wide slot. This is a knife big enough to be used as a weapon.

I scan the room.

The sink.

The knife is sitting on a cutting board next to the sink, ten feet away from us. A safe distance away.

I relax and exhale. I sit at the table, and I reach into my backpack and take out a ballpoint pen.

Jack's dad looks at me from the refrigerator, a question on his face.

"You taking notes?"

"When you talk baseball, I listen," I say.

Jack's dad smiles. I smile.

When in doubt, emulate.

I turn the cap until it clicks, exposing the point.

Jack's dad reaches forward to hand me the cold soda.

I push the end of the pen into the meat of his forearm. The action depresses a miniature plunger.

His eyes widen as the drug hits him. His mouth puckers, forming the familiar *Wh—*.

Maybe it's *why* he's trying to say.

Maybe it's *what*, as in *What are you doing?*

But the drug is fast-acting. Its actual speed depends on age and conditioning, which is bad news for Jack's dad.

He's out of shape.

So it is fast. Faster even than a word can form.

Jack's dad stumbles, and I catch him, place him on the floor by the kitchen table. I don't let him fall, because I don't want Jack running downstairs to see what caused the noise. I don't want anyone else rushing in. Not yet.

I need fifteen seconds.

Six seconds to lay him down, arranging the body, limbs splayed as if from a fall. I use an elbow to knock over the can of beer next to him. The foam hisses.

Five seconds to put away my pen and notebook, zip the backpack where it hangs from the back of a chair.

Four more seconds to play out the chain, let the chemical reaction in Mr. Wu's body take him beyond the point of resuscitation.

Fifteen seconds.

Done.

I look at the body. The man who was Chen Wu is gone.

A husband is gone.

A father is gone.

"I trust you," Jack said.

That was your mistake, I think.

Twenty seconds have passed. The outside edge of my operational window.

"Oh my god!" I say. "Help!"

I fling open the front door. "Someone!" I shout.

Jack comes running down the stairs, and his face turns white with shock. A sound comes out of him, something between a moan and a scream.

The security people rush in. One look at the body and the first guy knows.

It's all a show after that.

I stand to the side and watch it happen.

Resuscitation attempts, the ambulance, all of it.

I push forward like I want to be in the middle of the action, be near my friend Jack. The Suit from the baseball game stops me.

He puts an arm on my shoulder, gently, like he's my father or something. I want to shrug it off, but I don't.

"Maybe it would be better if you stepped away," he says.

"What about Jack—?"

"It's a family matter," he says.

I relax my shoulders beneath his arm.

"I need my backpack," I say.

He steps into the fray, grabs my backpack, hands it to me, and guides me out the door.

I glance back. My last image is of Jack on the sofa, his back hunched, his head almost to his knees.

A profile of grief.

All because of me.

I WALK PAST THE REVOLVING LIGHTS OF THE AMBULANCE.

Past the security vehicles, the police officers, the chatter of voices over shortwave radios.

"Do you need a ride?" the gate guard says.

"I'm good," I say.

"Tough day," he says.

"Terrible," I say.

"It happened on my watch," he says, shaking his head. "But they can't blame me, right? I'm not God. I don't get to decide when and where."

Not true. You don't have to be God to decide when and where. You only have to take action and be willing to deal with the consequences.

"Take care of yourself," he says.

"I always do," I say.

He opens the gate for me, and I'm out.

I walk down the street slowly, like someone who is traumatized. But I'm not traumatized. I'm already thinking about what comes next. I'm reviewing my exit strategy.

And maybe, just for a moment, I'm thinking about Jack.

He was my best friend for four weeks.

But not anymore.

He might not like it much that I killed his father. Not that he'll know. The drug leaves no trace. Jack's dad had a heart attack. That's what the autopsy will show, if there is an autopsy. Strings will be pulled. Or the modern equivalent—computer keys pressed.

If an autopsy is done, it will show nothing at all.

Natural causes.

That's my specialty. People die around me, but it never seems like my fault. It seems like bad luck following good.

Good luck: You meet a great new friend at school.

Bad luck: A tragedy befalls your family.

The two don't ever seem connected, but they are.

Jack didn't know that when we became best friends a month ago. I slipped into his life easily, and now I'm slipping out just as easily.

I've broken another guy's heart, changed the course of his life. Lucky for me, I can do it and not feel it.

I don't feel anything.

Not true.

I feel cold, I feel hungry, I feel the fabric of a new shirt rubbing against my skin, and I feel gravel beneath my feet.

But those are sensations, not feelings.

I had feelings once, too. I think I did. But that was a long time ago.

That was *before*.

HIS NAME WAS MIKE.

And he was my best friend.

Or so I thought.

He was the new guy in school, but he didn't seem new. The minute he started, it seemed like he'd been there forever.

"What are you into?" he said the first time I talked to him.

"I like to read," I said.

I was twelve then, and I had so many books that my dad had to build a second bookcase in my room.

"You read that vampire stuff?" he said.

"No. Action, adventure. Sci-fi if it's good."

"Cool," he said. "Me, too."

It didn't feel strange when we became instant friends, like when you feel separated at birth. *A brother from another mother.* That's what they call it.

Within a week, we were inseparable. Within two, he was sleeping over at the house.

We stayed up late, defying my parents, talking about everything under the sun. We exchanged books. We talked about girls.

It was during that year that I noticed girls were wearing bras, and you could see through their shirts if the light was right. Mike taught me you should always let the girl get between you and the window on a sunny day because it improved your viewing options. I thought he was a genius.

Mike and me. Two twelve-year-old kids, laughing and shooting the crap, thrilled to have found a partner in crime in each other.

In hindsight, I should have found it strange that I never saw his house, never met his parents. He said his dad was a corporate lawyer who traveled for business. My dad was a professor and scientist who sometimes went to conferences, so I knew what he meant. Kind of.

His mom got overwhelmed, he said. She didn't like kids around.

My mom got overwhelmed, too. Not with guests, but with my dad. At the time, they'd been fighting for what seemed like months. I didn't know what it was about, but it was one of those fights that was going on even when it wasn't, even when everything was quiet.

It went on for so long it felt like our family was having a nervous breakdown.

I told all this to Mike.

He was my friend. It felt good to tell him, to confide in him.

I didn't know he was going to kill my parents.

THIS HAPPENS SOMETIMES WHEN I FINISH.

Memories come. I don't know why.

They go away eventually if I keep moving.

I'm a mile from Jack's now, walking down the street, moving toward my egress point. If all has gone as planned, I should be clear and on my way out of town.

Should be.

I'm not.

I sense it a moment before it happens. Something in the air shifts. Everyone has intuition, but not everyone knows how to listen to it. I've been trained to listen, to perceive small changes in the environment around me, to predict outcomes before they happen.

And I've been trained to react.

My intuition tells me something is about to happen.

And then it does.

A dark gray sedan comes around the corner. The car jerks

slightly when the driver sees me. It happens in a split second, like when someone spots a pothole at the last moment and pulls the wheel to avoid it.

But there's no pothole. Only me.

It's a natural human reaction. When you spot what you're looking for, your body reacts. In poker they call it a *tell*, a physical tic that reveals what's going on with the player.

This driver has a tell. That's good.

Because by the time the car pulls to a stop in the middle of the road, I've had a few seconds to prepare.

I rapid-scan the area:

Empty road behind. Stone and gravel surface beneath. A spattering of houses set way back from the road, their views obscured behind thickets of trees.

And the car in front of me, twenty yards away.

I continue for a few steps, and the license comes into view. It's not one of Jack's dad's cars. This car has diplomatic plates.

The doors open. Four Asian men in suits get out. They do it casually, as if the non sequitur of four men in suits stopped in the middle of a suburban street is no big deal.

Choices:

I could escape into the woods. See how good they are on foot and separated.

Some would say that's the best strategy in this situation, divide power and take it on little by little.

Some say that. I don't.

There's another trick that I learned from the people who trained me. Don't diffuse power; concentrate it. Get it too close together, where its effectiveness is reduced.

That's the trick I will use.

The problem: I never carry a gun, and my weaponized ballpoint pen and other tools were dropped down a sewer. I left my empty backpack in a Dumpster a ways down the road.

So I've got nothing to rely on but my training.

It should be enough.

But I can't know for sure.

I stay on the same trajectory, moving toward the car. Ten yards away now. I keep my posture nonthreatening. I'm a sixteen-year-old kid walking down the street. That's what I want them to see.

It's also the truth. I am sixteen. I am walking.

As I get closer, I can hear the men talking to one another in Mandarin. I see the cheap material of their suits, and I see how their jackets fit poorly over bulky shoulders.

Diplomats do not have bulky shoulders. Maybe one guy if he's into fitness. Not four in a row.

I don't know these guys. I didn't come across them on the assignment with Jack. But they know something about me because they're looking at me like I'm dinner at the zoo.

This could get interesting real fast.

"Hey," the first one says. "We're lost. Can you give us directions?"

His English is good. His ploy is not.

Nobody stops his car on a diagonal in the middle of the road to ask for directions.

It's ridiculous, but I'm a teenager, so people often underestimate me.

Most teenagers fight against that because they want to prove how tough they are.

Not me.

It's good to be underestimated. It's what's known as a tactical advantage.

So when the Chinese guy asks for directions, I say, "Sure. Where are you headed?"

He's a little surprised, but not totally.

Still underestimating.

"I've got the address on my phone," he says.

He holds out an Android phone for me to look at. The guy next to him shifts his eyes toward it. The phone is arm's length away. Which means I have to come within arm's length to read it.

I move closer.

The two guys in the back step in, tightening the net. They relax at the same time. *This is going to be easy.* That's what they're thinking. I see it reflected in their posture.

Two rows of two. I'm walking toward them and putting the story together at the same time. Thick chests, tight haircuts, and diplomatic plates. I'm probably looking at Chinese spies. I'm guessing Jack's father was in business with them, and that's the reason I was sent here.

But I don't know for sure. I don't need to know.

Asking questions is not what I do. I'm given an assignment, and I carry it out.

Most of the time it's simple, but something has gone wrong, because they're here, and I've been detected.

I'll save the questions for later.

Only one thing matters right now.

Survive.

I do not fight for sport. I fight when it is necessary.

If they get me in a car with diplomatic plates, it's all over. There will be no police interference, no help for me at all.

I cannot let that happen.

The guy who spoke English holds out his phone to me. I think of one of those deep-sea fish that has an appendage dangling in front of its mouth to attract prey. A fish with its own fishing rod, designed by nature.

AP Biology, Subtopic 3C: Competition and Predation.

This guy has his phone. He dangles it.

I take the bait.

Literally take it. Out of his hands.

I twirl and smash the phone into the bridge of his nose. I don't ask questions, and I don't hesitate. Not against four men.

The glass shatters. His nose shatters.

Before he even hits the ground, I'm on to the next man. This time it's the corner of the phone. I spin and swing, and he takes it in the left eye. A quick adjustment, and I stab the phone into his right eye. The globe resists briefly before rupturing.

Two down.

Surprise was my advantage. No more.

The third man comes. He's bigger than the others. Much bigger. He guards his face as he moves. He won't be fooled like his friends.

So I fool him another way.

Noting that the fourth man has cleared to the edge of the road, I dive for the open car door. It's exactly where number three wanted me a minute ago. But a minute is a long time in a fight. He thought he'd be putting me in the backseat. The fact that I'm already there means he has to come after me.

I move as though I'm going to jump through the door and out the other side.

I do half of that. I get into the car. I don't get out again.

He comes.

It's a narrow space. Flexibility wins over bulk in a narrow space.

I'm flexibility. He's bulk.

He tries to get his arms around to swing at me, but there's not enough room.

I still have the phone. This time I tuck it in my fist to weight the punch, and I lash out hard three times.

It stuns him but doesn't disable him.

I slip out, and when he comes after me, I bash the door into his face.

He drops to the ground, out cold.

He knows how to take a punch, but he doesn't know how to take a car door to the head. Nobody does.

I look up to find the fourth man waiting with his gun out.

He's got a gun, and I've got a broken phone in my hand.

Not what you'd call a fair fight.

A stupid guy with a gun would think he'd already won. Not the fourth man. He's smart. He's been watching and learning.

He stays far away from the phone, away from me and outside of my striking range.

He keeps the gun aimed at my center mass. Which means he knows how to use it. If you aim at someone's head and they move quickly, there's very little chance you're going to hit them. Not so if you keep the weapon on center mass.

I don't use guns, but I know all about them. At least enough to know that I'm screwed.

He motions with his head for me to turn around. Doesn't wave the gun barrel like an inexperienced man would do.

If I turn now, I've lost.

I don't think he's going to shoot me. He's going to take me somewhere and ask questions. That's a lot worse than being shot.

I think of my father. The last time I saw him I was twelve years old. He was taped to a chair and bleeding. Someone had asked him questions.

Questions are bad.

That day with my father was a long time ago. Another time, another life.

Now there is a man with a gun.

Now I must look for options.

Now I must survive.

The fourth man shouts at me in Mandarin. I don't know what he's saying, but he's angry. He knows what I'm trying to do. Stall. Work the angles. And with three of his colleagues down and bleeding, he's not treating me like a sixteen-year-old anymore.

I look at the gun. I look at his eyes.

Cold.

I'm in trouble.

And then the phone rings.

The Android phone in my hand. The glass is shattered, but the phone is still working.

The ring surprises him as much as it surprises me.

Surprise is not a bad thing. Not if you can use it to your advantage.

I answer the phone.

"*Ni hao ma?*" I say. *How are you?* in Chinese.

That's about all I know how to say.

I listen to the phone for a moment, then I hold it out to the fourth man as if it's for him. He's so shocked he doesn't know what to do.

I shake the phone a little. I look at him like he's an idiot. We both hear the man shouting over the phone, his voice tinny and distant.

I don't know what he's saying, but it doesn't matter.

AP Bio, Subtopic 3C.

I dangle the phone in front of me.

The guy reaches—

And I hit him in the head, in the soft spot of his right temple, an inch behind his eye. I hit so hard that the phone comes apart in my hand.

He drops to the ground.

Done.

What if the phone didn't ring? What would have happened?

Not now. I can't think about that now.

"Chance can be your friend or your enemy," Mother used to say. "Make it a friend."

Mother, that's what I call the woman who trained me.

She'd taught me this lesson, and I applied it today.

I look at the bodies of the four men on the ground around me. I look at the gun by my feet.

Mother taught me another lesson. Death is a tool I use for my work. It's not something I do lightly. I could finish these men, but it is not strictly necessary. They are already crippled, their mission thwarted.

They do not need to die. At least not now.

Issue closed.

It's time to use a real phone. My iPhone.

It looks like a normal phone, but it's not. The physical architecture is the same, but the operating system is much different. And the apps? Well, they're far from average.

I open the Weather Channel app. I click on REPORT HAZARDOUS CONDITIONS.

I hold up the phone. A map appears with a GPS dot that shows my position. It glows red, then a second later flashes green.

A cleanup crew will be here shortly.

Mother will not be happy. I might have some explaining to do.

I take the car keys from the fourth man's pocket. I start up the sedan. It's not like Chinese spies are going to report a stolen car.

Besides, it's got diplomatic plates. And I like to drive fast.

I'M SPEEDING DOWN THE PIKE.

I'd never do it under normal circumstances. Nothing to draw attention to myself.

But diplomatic plates and driving like an asshole go hand in hand. Besides, I'm on the Pike, where traffic laws are optional.

I'm heading toward Boston now, putting distance between myself and the incident. The mile markers tick by, each one making me safer than the last.

I glance in my rearview, automatically scanning for tails. I open the sunroof so I can monitor the sky.

I'm alone.

I briefly think of Jack, what it's like for him right now. In a split second he's become a sad statistic. His father's death will be a minor tragedy among the privileged students at Natick Prep. A young man, the unexpected loss of a parent, a period of mourning, a period of adjustment.

But I know something Jack doesn't know:

Life goes on.

Even after the worst of tragedies, it just keeps going.

I am sixteen, but this is an old lesson to me. It helps me do what I must do.

There is something else I know:

Jack's father was not who he seemed to be.

Jack thought of his father as the CEO of a tech firm with high-level government contracts.

That much was true.

But his father was something else, too. He was secretly working with the wrong people. After dancing with four Chinese spies this afternoon, I'm guessing it was the Chinese government.

The details are not for me to know. They are not my business.

My business is to get in, do the job, and get out again. Move on to the next.

The job is assigned to me.

I don't have to think. I have to act.

The general picture, that's all I need, and the true picture of Jack's father is that he was doing something he was not supposed to be doing. Something that made him dangerous, possibly even a traitor.

That's why I was sent here. To stop him.

It's my specialty. I get an assignment, and I carry it out.

The Program, the organization I work for, says I am a patriot, but patriots have a choice. I do not.

Maybe that's not true.

I had a choice a long time ago, and I made a mistake.

My father had a choice, too. He chose wrong, or I wouldn't be here.

Back to Jack and his father. The matter at hand.

I don't need to have an opinion about what I've done, but I do have a way of thinking about it that helps me.

I've done Jack a favor.

He doesn't know the damage his father has already done or the damage he was yet to do if he were not stopped.

Unlike me, Jack's cherished image of his father will be maintained forever, frozen in time. Who and what his father was will never be known. Not to him. Not to anyone.

Here's what Jack will remember:

The beautiful lie that defined his family.

I am not lucky like Jack.

I know the truth about my family. Or some of it.

I know my father was not the great dad I thought he was, or the man he pretended to be to the world. The Program tells me one thing, but my memories tell me another.

I don't know which to believe.

It's enough to make all my memories suspect, to make the past a mystery from which I cannot escape.

I was twelve years old.

I was waiting for my father in his office at the university, and I got a call. There had been an accident, and I had to come home immediately. That's what the caller said.

I ran home to find Mike sitting at our kitchen table. I was surprised to see him there.

"Where are my parents?" I said.

There were cookies on a plate in the middle of the table. Oatmeal raisin. Mom used to put them out for us. I was skinny and hardly ate. Mike was big for his age and ate a lot.

"Your parents," Mike said. "I need to talk to you about them."

I noticed a can of diet ginger ale on the floor by the refrigerator. It had spilled and formed a sticky brown-yellow puddle. I was looking at it, wondering how it got there, wondering why nobody had done anything about it, when Mike reached out and touched me with something.

Something sharp, like a thumbtack.

I suddenly felt tired.

"Don't be afraid," he said to me.

"Why would I be afraid?" I said.

My head started to spin, and I fell. Mike steadied me. He propped me against his shoulder and led me into the living room. A friend helping another friend in distress.

My father was sitting on a chair in the living room, his head slumped in front of him, his legs duct-taped to the legs of the chair.

"That's funny," I said.

When you see something absurd, something that is beyond your power to comprehend, your mind interprets it as a joke. It is a natural human defense mechanism. I've used it to my advantage many times.

I didn't know things like that back then. I was young and stupid. I thought we were playing a game.

"It is funny," Mike said. "Funny and sad."

"I don't understand," I said.

Mike snapped his fingers hard. Once, twice.

My dad's head shot up. He could not speak. There was tape over his mouth.

"Dad," I said.

His eyes told the story.

This was no game. It was danger.

Mike grabbed the back of my collar, pulled me close to my father, so close we were almost touching.

"Do you see?" Mike said.

But he wasn't talking to me.

I was only twelve, but I understood. I might not have been able to put it into words at the time, but I got the idea.

Mike hadn't brought me to the living room to show me what he'd done to my father; he'd brought me there to show my father what he was going to do to me.

"This is not your son," Mike told my father. "Not anymore."

I tried to reach out to my father, but Mike pulled me away.

I was more than tired then. I was falling asleep on my feet.

"Who are you?" I said to Mike.

"I'm your friend," he said. "I'm Mike."

"You're not my friend," I said.

"You're a smart kid," he said.

The way he'd said it, it was like he wasn't a kid. He was something else, something I didn't yet know existed.

He led me outside. I had no ability to resist. He put me in the back of a waiting cab. It looked like a cab, but the windows were blacked out.

That was the last time I saw either of my parents.

It was the end of everything.

It was the beginning of everything else.

I STEP ON THE GAS AND FEEL THE ENGINE RESPOND.

I look out the window as mile markers pass in a blur. Buildings in a blur. Faces in a blur. I learned long ago that the world is blurred by speed. The greater the speed, the more the blur.

If I keep moving forward, it will stay that way.

The thought makes me breathe easier.

When I'm ten miles away from the primary zone, I see the Dunkin' Donuts up ahead.

I pull into the big parking lot, and I leave the sedan in a far corner. It's a beast. I hate to see it go.

I switch to the car that's waiting for me here. A Camry, complete with a scratched rear bumper and dented hubcaps. Designed to blend. Boring. Slow.

I take out my iPhone. I slide the bar to the left, up, then quickly down and up on the diagonal. It's a custom gesture that puts the phone in secure mode.

I open the Games folder, click on the Poker app. Click NEW GAME.

The cards shuffle.

I arrange a hand of ten cards, a phone number's worth, and I click DEAL.

The computer opens a connection to an anonymous server. My voice is converted to a digital signal, chopped up into packets, sent across the Web, and reassembled.

A complex process that takes no more than a second.

One beep tone, and a woman answers.

"Hello, Mom," I say.

That's what I call this woman. Mother. The woman who is in charge of everything. Father runs my assignments. Mother oversees.

Mother and Father. That's how I refer to the people who manage me. We do it for security purposes. If for some reason our secure line were breached, you'd hear nothing but a mother talking to her son.

Her son.

That's what she calls me.

"Sweetheart," the voice on the phone says. She sounds like a person who's happy to get my call. "I heard about the game from your father."

"Then you know I won," I say.

"I do."

"But there were—complications. Afterward, I mean."

Silence.

"Four troublemakers," I say. "Unexpected."

"To you. Not to me."

I'm glad she knew about the Chinese spies but troubled by the fact that I didn't. Could I have missed something?

"Can you tell me anything else about who they were?" I say. "It might help me do a better job next time."

"I was told they were spectators at the game, and they wandered onto the field. Wrong place, wrong time."

"So there's nothing to worry about?"

"Nothing at all," Mother says.

"I'm relieved," I say.

Traffic zooms by on the Pike. I look across the road at a giant billboard. A smiling family sits at a kitchen table eating dinner.

Home is where the ♥ is.

That's what the sign says. The heart has steam wafting from the top.

It makes no sense to me.

I study it for a moment, trying to understand the meaning.

"You won your game," Mother says. "That's what matters. Your father and I are very proud of you."

"Really?"

"Absolutely," she says.

Proud.

It's nice to hear. It means I've done my job well, completed another assignment. I was even able to adjust to unforeseen circumstances at the end.

I'm good at what I do, and I'm appreciated for it. So why is there a question nagging at me?

When does it end?

That's what I want to know.

My life is one continual assignment. I move from world to world as I've been trained to do, leaving nothing but bodies behind me. With each assignment comes new challenges, new complications, new excitement.

You have a gift. That's what Mother once told me. She said she saw it in me the first day we met.

I'm lucky that way. How many sixteen-year-olds know who they are or what they're supposed to be doing in the world?

Yet with all I know and all I've been taught, still the question comes:

When does it end?

I think about promises that were made. The lies I was told.

No, I correct myself. Not lies.

Promises that I misunderstood.

I was young then. How could I have known?

MIKE PUT ME IN THE TAXI.

I do not remember the ride.

Mike had drugged me. Drugged me but not killed me. He could have done either. I know that now. It was simply a matter of which syringe he chose. One click is death. Two clicks is temporary coma.

I woke up in a beautiful bedroom with sunlight streaming through the window.

I yawned and stretched, thinking it was vacation, and we were in the house in South Carolina that my father rented for a month every summer.

I looked out the window at a forest I did not recognize.

This wasn't South Carolina.

Memories flooded back, rising up from my narcotic haze.

My father taped to the chair. The look of terror in his eyes.

I ran to the bedroom door.

It was locked.

I screamed.

I flung myself against it.

I ran to the window, and it, too, was locked.

I tried to crack the glass, but it was unbreakable.

I screamed some more. I flung myself against walls. I destroyed furniture.

Eventually the door opened.

The woman I would later know as Mother stood there calmly looking at me.

"Where are my parents?" I said.

"Dead."

That was the first word I ever heard out of her mouth. I didn't know that death would become the basis of our relationship.

She sat me down, and she gave me a choice. I could join my parents, or I could join her. Join The Program.

That's what she called it. The Program.

She described it to me in the most basic terms. I would become a soldier. I would be trained physically and mentally. I would do things most boys do only in video games.

She made it sound exciting.

She said it was my choice whether to join.

Whatever I decided, my life was no longer my own. I could give it up forever and join my parents, or I could join The Program.

Twelve years old, and I had to make a choice between life and death.

I chose death.

Call it loyalty. Call it naïveté.

I wanted to be with my parents, even if it meant dying.

So this is what I told her:

"Kill me."

Ironically, it was what they were looking for. It showed them the level of character they were seeking, the list of personality characteristics appropriate to a potential soldier.

Intensity.

Black-or-white thinking.

Stubbornness.

Allegiance without regard to consequence.

All useful qualities from their perspective. They took my allegiance and transformed it into something that would serve them.

Serve The Program.

Mother promised me a new life.

That's what I got.

I CAN HEAR MOTHER BREATHING ON THE OTHER END OF THE PHONE.

"Are you there?" she says.

"I'm here."

"I said we're proud of you."

"I appreciate that."

It's my cue. I'm supposed to say good-bye and hang up, but I don't. The silence on the line grows uncomfortable.

"Anything else, honey?" the voice says.

There is an edge to it now.

When? my head screams.

"Nothing else," I say. "I'm just anxious to get to the next assignment."

The question goes away when I get an assignment. The question, the memories, all of it.

"Keep an eye on your e-mail," Mother says. "Your father is sending you something."

That's how the assignments come. Through Father.

"I'll get it soon?"

"You know your father. He moves at his own pace."

"Of course."

"You're sure you're okay?" she says.

"Why wouldn't I be?"

The briefest of pauses, and Mother says, "I have to run now. Lots of love."

"Love you. Talk to you soon," I say.

Back to the script. When in doubt, stick to the script.

The line goes dead.

I close the Poker app.

On the billboard the mother smiles warmly behind perfectly made-up lips. Her son lifts a spoonful of hot liquid to his mouth. She looks on proudly.

Home is where the ♥ is.

Home. Is that what home looks like?

I stare at the billboard.

Suddenly the meaning becomes clear.

There is nothing deep about it. It's an ad for soup.

THE WAITING.

That is the most difficult part.

There is the assignment I have finished, and the assignment to come. In between is a black hole called waiting.

I cannot go back to Natick now. The house where I lived has already been sanitized, and the story of why I had to leave has been seeded. I was living there alone for two months while my parents were on an extended business trip.

That was the establishing story.

There was a terrible accident overseas. I had to leave without notice.

That's the exit story.

Now it's time to change cities and wait. In this case, the black hole is called Providence.

I travel by train whenever possible. It's slow and old-fashioned, but that can work in my favor. Lax security, no ID checks, and it's easy to buy a ticket under an assumed name. Besides, I enjoy it. I feel safest encased in metal and in motion.

I take the Acela Express train and in less than an hour I'm checking into the Marriott in downtown Providence. A hotel can be tricky when you're sixteen years old. I have adult IDs and credit cards, but I have to be careful with my choice of clothes. I can't walk in looking like a teenager. There will be questions.

They don't care about me. They care about the room. They're afraid a teenager will have a party and trash it. He'll get drunk and pass out, and they'll have a liability issue.

Sometimes I'll call ahead and reserve the room for my son, but that requires a story, and stories invite attention.

Stories can be remembered. A regular check-in cannot.

So I keep it standard as much as possible. Big cities are best. Chains are best. Clubs are best. I'm a Marriott Rewards member under ten names.

I walk toward the front desk. A large group stands around in front of the restaurant, an eclectic mix of people from their twenties to their fifties, excited and chattering. They have that happy look like they've been sprung from prison.

I glance at the conference announcements.

WELCOME, LIBRARIANS! one of the signs reads.

"Are you one of us?" a well-dressed woman with funky glasses says.

"Wish I was," I say.

That earns me a big smile.

I walk to the front desk and pass the clerk my credit card. She swipes it and slides it toward me on the counter.

"Welcome back, Mr. Gallant," the clerk says.

She glances at me. A questioning look. *Aren't you a little young to be Mr. Gallant?*

A kid would say, *Mr. Gallant is my father.* Try to prove he's cool.

"A pleasure to be back," I say. Act older. Look older.

"Will it be a long stay?"

"If I'm lucky, it will be a short one," I say.

"Maybe you'll find something in Providence you like."

She smiles at me, and I look at her closely for the first time—dark hair, smoky eyes, and a black fitted uniform that can't hide a great body underneath.

We might have fun together, but I can't afford the distraction. Instead of taking advantage of the opening she's given me, I make light of it.

"Is there anything in Providence that anyone likes?" I say.

She laughs.

"You should know you're insulting my hometown," she says.

"Looks like I just got a room with a view of the parking lot."

I put the focus back on the room, the check-in process.

Business. That's all this is.

"I'm not like that," she says.

She types on the computer for a second. She glances up at me.

"Truth is we've got a lot of great things to do in this town. If you're interested, I could show you a few of the hot spots."

Changing the subject didn't work. It's time to be direct.

"I'm interested," I say, "but I don't have time. It's just a quick business trip."

"That's a shame."

"It really is."

She passes me a small paper envelope with my key card.

"Room seven fifty-nine. A nice view. I guarantee it."

"Thank you."

I don't look at her name tag. Better not to say her name. Better not to create any more connection between us.

Connections can be remembered. As such, they are dangerous to me.

I nod and step aside, let another guest fill my spot. Maybe he'll do what I cannot, hit the hot spots, enjoy his trip to Providence.

Connect.

I look at the envelope with the key card.

Room 759. This is where I will wait.

I TAKE OFF MY CLOTHES.

I put them in a plastic bag, put that inside my travel bag. I'll drop the plastic bag in a Goodwill bin later. Not a Dumpster. A bag of clothes in a Dumpster invites speculation.

I look at my naked body in the mirror.

When I'm dressed, I'm average in all ways.

Naked, my body tells a different story.

There is the physique. But that can be explained by high school athletics. Most of the time I keep five extra pounds on me to camouflage my muscles.

The problem with being naked is the scar. It's an ugly gash, hard with scar tissue, located on my left pec in the meat between my chest and shoulder.

A knife wound.

I touch it now, explore the region of dead flesh with my fingers.

Mother calls bad experiences *teachable moments*. Life lessons.

I had a teachable moment that left its mark on me forever. I learned a lot from this particular one. I learned that facing a person with a knife focuses the mind, even more so when he is pressing the knife into your chest, two inches of the blade disappearing into your flesh.

I learned that Mike was capable of anything.

You learn many things with a knife in your shoulder.

You learn how to save your life. Or how to die.

But that's what it means to be a soldier. You train for situations like that, and you hope that when they arrive—if they arrive—you will be ready.

THE FIRST TWO YEARS IN THE PROGRAM WERE PREPARATION.

Two years to change me from a boy into something else. Human alchemy as practiced by The Program.

At first I fought the transformation. Then I went with it.

My initial impulse to die went away quickly. Nobody really wants to die. It's unnatural. What I was really experiencing was shock. My parents' death, my betrayal by Mike, my captivity with strangers.

When the shock passed, my desire to die was replaced by a more natural instinct.

The desire to live.

I threw myself into the training.

There were no other kids training with me. There were only me and a group of professionals. All of them adults.

An entire program created for me, or so it seemed at the time.

I felt special.

Father coordinated. Mother appeared at intervals to check my progress.

There were academics. All of high school and beyond in less than two years.

There was physical training. Weapons and tactics.

There were strategy and psychology.

And there were tests. Many, many tests. Not the kind an average kid has to take. Tests of my courage, my stamina, my fighting skills, my ability to adjust to surprise.

These were the kinds of tests that are graded Pass/Fail. And Fail in The Program means you do not walk away.

When they deemed me ready, there was an explanation of my new job.

Only they didn't call it a job. They called it a mission.

I am a patriot. That's what I was told.

As such, my only true job is allegiance to The Program, which gave me life, and to the country I serve.

There may be more like me. Teens hidden in schools across the land, doing what I do. Getting close. Then completing their assignments.

If they exist, I've not met them.

There's only one other like me, as far as I know.

Mike. The boy who killed my parents.

The boy I had to fight in order to graduate.

I RUN MY FINGER OVER THE HARD RIDGE OF THE SCAR.

Remembering Mike, my brother in The Program. And hating him.

I tell myself I was unskilled then. Not unskilled, exactly, but inexperienced.

Not like today.

Today it would be different.

But even then I learned the lesson:

Survive.

I flip on the television in the hotel room, reaching for some distraction.

This is the problem with waiting. Time to think, time to remember. It's not helpful to me.

I scan the local news.

Somewhere in Massachusetts, an important Chinese businessman had a heart attack. It makes the regional news down in Providence.

I watch a news cycle on CNN. It does not make national.

The lead story is about the new peace initiative in the Middle East, threatened yet again by violence. The Israeli prime minister and his government are seeking a lasting peace in the region, but elements in his own government are opposing the idea. Shots of a rubble-strewn street in Jerusalem, the blast where a bomb has destroyed a storefront. The Israeli prime minister, well known for his moderate views, begging for calm.

I change over to MTV.

A show about teen dating.

It's supposed to be a reality show, but it is not. I can see that the people are lying. They have memorized their lines.

This is what I've been taught:

If you want to know if someone is lying, turn down the volume. In real life that means stop listening to what they're saying and watch their actions.

People will say anything. But the things they do—that's the real tell.

I turn down the volume on the television.

I look at the teens on the show, all smiles and white teeth, mouths opening and closing in a pantomime of love.

I think about my father. Not the man whose e-mail I wait for. My real father.

I think of him coming home from work when I was a boy. What he wore, the briefcase he carried. I think of the day he brought me to work at the University of Rochester and introduced me to his colleagues.

I was young then. I trusted. I believed.

No more.

Questionable loyalty. That's what Mother told me when I got to The Program. I asked her why I had been brought there, and she said, "Your father had questionable loyalty."

She said it like it was damning, like my father had wavered in his allegiance. To what or whom, I don't know.

In my memory, I turn down the volume and I watch my father at the university. I see him speaking to his colleagues, his mouth moving, no sound coming. I watch as he introduces me. I look into his eyes. I watch as he passes a security card through a locked door and brings me into the research lab. I remember how important I felt, how lucky to be in this place where no guests are allowed. My father was special. He had privileges.

I scan his office. I try to understand who he was and what he was doing.

If not a professor, then what?

If not a research scientist, then what?

If not a good man, then what?

I run the scene again and again in my mind, but I don't find anything questionable.

Only my father, telling the truth in the month before he died.

THREE DAYS PASS.

Three long days in Providence. I sleep, I work out, I go to the movies alone.

Mostly, I wait.

I do not establish patterns, and I make no friends.

It's Tuesday morning when a chime wakes me from a restless sleep.

I roll over and check my phone.

An e-mail from The Program.

Check out this video. Funny!!!
Dad

Funny. Three exclamation marks.

That's code for an urgent communication. I remember this from my operational training, but it's never been used before.

Something critical needs my attention. A new assignment.

It is beginning again.

At last.

I ORDER A LARGE COFFEE AT THE LOCAL STARBUCKS.

"You want to add a shot to that?" the barista says.

"Why do you ask?"

"You look like a man on a mission. A little pick-me-up couldn't hurt."

I look at the barista, monitoring his face for anything out of the ordinary that would suggest he knows who I am. If need be, I could leap over the counter and be on him in an instant.

"It's just a shot," he says. "What doesn't kill you makes you stronger."

He smiles. I smile.

I can see now that he's harmless. I'm misreading the situation. Maybe the Chinese spies shook me up a little. Or maybe it's the waiting. No matter. I've got business to attend to.

"Make it two shots," I say to the barista.

"My man," he says.

I find an empty chair in the very rear of the store, and I log on to the free Wi-Fi.

I can make my phone secure, but for assignment instructions, it's safer to have another layer of anonymity between me and the world. Nothing more anonymous than a local Starbucks.

I've been taught a few simple tricks, all of them the same trick. Hide in plain sight.

It's the best way to make yourself invisible.

My phone logs on with a fake Mac ID, the phone's version of a social security number. I settle in and open Father's e-mail again.

Check out this video. Funny!!!
Dad

The e-mail is followed by a link to YouTube. There's also an image to download. A tiny image. Barely 5K in size. The image is nothing special—a picture of a mountain lake. As if my father had been on vacation and uploaded a snapshot at extremely low quality.

The photo means nothing at all, but the size means everything.

5K. Five days.

That is the operational window for my next assignment.

It can't be right.

I check the photo again to make sure I read the number correctly.

5K. No mistake.

My job is always the same: Enter, gain trust, integrate, and complete my assignment. All without being noticed.

This is not a quick process. It takes one to three months, depending on a whole number of factors.

Five days. What is that?

I look around the Starbucks. Lots of people on laptops. An old couple chatting. Two cute girls in workout clothes laughing.

Nobody paying attention to me.

I click on the YouTube link. The video is nothing at all. A famous band, the lead singer of which falls off the stage mid-ballad. Maybe it's funny, but that's beside the point. I scan down until I get to the sixteenth comment.

First word = **S**ucks.

Last word = **G**o.

SG. The initials of the Facebook profile for me to locate.

When I log into Facebook, I find over a dozen new friend requests, but only one of them from a guy named EssGee in New York City.

SG. That is the one that requires my attention.

This is not a real profile, of course. It has not been created by EssGee, and when it is removed after I'm done, it will not be removed by him.

It's not a profile at all, but a dossier.

I accept the friend request and click on the link to his profile.

The real name of the person is at the top.

SG. Sam Goldberg.

First surprise: Sam is a girl.

I do not like dealing with girls. They are complicated.

I am equally effective with girls and guys, but girls create another level of difficulty. More emotion, more problems.

Second surprise: Sam is pretty. More than pretty. Beautiful.

She looks vaguely Middle Eastern, shoulder-length curly hair, long and thin with high cheekbones, ample in her chest.

I don't care about beauty itself. But beauty means boys. Suitors. Jealousy. Competition. Beauty can make my job more difficult.

I look at Sam's photo.

There is something familiar about her. A distant alarm goes off in my head.

At a nearby table, the girls in workout clothes laugh. Their teeth are very white.

I breathe. I focus. The alarm in my head gets quiet.

Back to the profile.

Two photo albums. The first is my mark.

I click on it.

Photos of Sam.

Jumping in the air on a trampoline, her face frozen in joy.

Sam at a Model UN conference, her face intense as she argues at a podium.

Sam and three friends messing around at a dance, each of them putting a leg in the arm of another.

The intimacies of this girl's life spread out in front of me like a deck of cards.

I feel a vague sense of discomfort, spying on an innocent girl.

Then I remember: Nobody is innocent.

Still, there is something familiar about this girl. What is it?

I click the next photo. Sam and friends posed in front of the facade of an unusual building in Manhattan. The shape is something like a giant television screen. I recognize the name of an exclusive private school on the Upper West Side.

I move to photo album two. The critical album.

First photo. Sam dressed for a formal event of some kind. A black-tie dinner. Unusual for a teen to be attending. But maybe not for a wealthy teen in Manhattan.

Sam is elegant in black. Younger than in the previous photos. This is from a few years ago.

Next photo. Sam posed with her parents at that same event.

My eyes widen. My breathing quickens.

I double-click to enlarge the photo. I have to be sure I'm seeing it correctly.

Sam is in the same black dress between her father and mother, their arms around one another. Her father looks delighted, completely at ease in front of the camera.

He should be. He's the mayor of New York.

NOW I KNOW WHERE I'VE SEEN HER BEFORE.

Samara Goldberg, daughter of Mayor Goldberg.

They call him the West Side Mayor. A mayor of the people. A mayor both elevated and grounded, still connected to his roots.

Jonathan Goldberg is a former mathematical statistician and professor. His analytical theories made him a fortune as owner of a global security research firm. Pulled into politics somewhat against his will. Rose quickly after that.

The mayor is tall and skinny in the photo, stretched long like his daughter. Older than Sam's mother by quite a few years. Her mother is a beauty. I can see where Sam gets her looks.

I remember the story now. Sam's mother died several years ago—an accident while she was visiting family in Israel. A freak accident. Wrong place, wrong time.

Afterward the mayor went into mourning, along with the city that loves him.

My heart is beating too fast. One hundred forty bpm. High for me.

I stand and stretch. The girls look over at me. Why is a guy stretching out in the middle of Starbucks?

"Still hurting from my workout," I say.

One of the girls giggles and whispers to her friend.

I'm attracting too much attention. I sit back down, pull in my energy. I breathe deeply, slow the rate of my pulse.

I click the photo so it becomes small again. I count back in the order.

I've looked at two photos, but it's the third photo that is important.

Second album, third photo. That is always the target.

It could be anyone. An uncle or aunt. Even a nanny. Anyone close to the family.

I click on photo three.

It's a picture of Mayor Goldberg. Alone.

He is the target.

Sam is the mark, the mayor of New York is the target, and five days is my timeline.

That is my new assignment.

I check on the barista again. He's working the bar now, his face obscured behind a layer of steam.

It's time to go.

I grasp the phone in one palm and slam the left corner down on the table. One time, sharply and at a particular angle.

The girls look in my direction and frown. I must look like an angry kid, making a bad choice with his phone. But that's not what's happening. It's a built-in fail-safe.

When I hit the phone, the accelerometer measures the exact angle and force of the blow and sends a signal to the battery that causes it to overheat, destroying the interior of the phone.

A block away I drop the dead phone into a covered trash can, and I get on a train bound for New York.

As the wheels sing beneath me, I think about the difficult assignment ahead. I wonder how I will do it in five days.

It will be a challenge, no doubt.

But challenges are what I'm best at.

It begins.

I appear at a famous private school on the Upper West Side.

Sam's school.

The Program has inserted me into the system overnight. I am in the school's computer—my name and a false academic history along with a letter of acceptance and a transfer order. As of this morning, my paperwork is in place and I will appear on the teachers' rosters.

The rest is up to me.

I'm sitting in a cluster group, what other schools would call a homeroom. There are mixed ages in the same room, students from grades nine through twelve, all forced together.

Sam is in a nearby room, but I am here. By design.

First impressions are everything in high school, but without knowing Sam, I don't know what my first impression should be. I could come in guns blazing, an ironclad identity in place. But that would be too much of a risk. First I have to find out where she is in the pecking order. The daughter of the mayor could be many things. To determine what exactly, I must see her in action. I need to know where she is in the social order, and just as importantly, where she perceives herself to be.

Father and I discussed this via a secure e-mail exchange. He agreed that it's better for me to slip in, work the angles until I'm on the inside. We decided to place me in a different cluster group so I could get my bearings before I begin.

"Are you new?" a girl in the cluster group says. She's in the seat next to mine, a mass of bangs with two overly done eyes staring out at me from beneath. A junior by the looks of it.

"Newish," I say.

"Why haven't I seen you before?"

I glance over her shoulder at a boy. Athletic, a tight chest. She's been sneaking glances at him for the last ten minutes.

"Because you're obsessed with him," I say, pointing to the guy.

She turns bright red.

"That's not funny," she says.

I shrug.

Conversation over.

I hear a soft chuckle from two rows behind me.

It's a younger guy, maybe fourteen years old, pale with uncombed hair. Definition of *dork*. Watching.

"Good one," he says.

"Thanks," I say.

"You transferred to a new school in April," he says. "Who did you piss off?"

"I got kicked out of Choate."

"You must have really screwed up."

I shrug and go back to reading a book.

Let the rumors commence. It's a good way to start, inject some mystery into my story. Later I can spin it in a hundred different ways, turn myself into a troubled kid, a victim, or a rebel—whatever is most effective.

For now, I trust this pale kid will let it slip. And I mark him as someone to monitor. I have to be careful with guys who are outsiders. They watch. There's nothing much else for them to do.

Ten minutes go by as I study the cluster group. I watch the patterns, the behavior, the styles of dress. I listen to the rhythm of the language in this new place. I learn the school procedures. I soak it all in.

At five past eight, three soft tones sound a few seconds apart, and the students stand up.

It's time to meet Sam.

IT IS JUST ANOTHER DAY TO THEM.

That's why it's preferable to start midweek. No excitement. Expectations are low.

Today happens to be Wednesday. I like Wednesday. It's the day I might have chosen anyway if there had been more time.

I look at people in the halls. Yawning, rubbing their eyes, still waking up.

Unaware.

In a big public school I might stay below the radar for days, making myself invisible until I choose to emerge. Not here. Private school classes are too small, and the time frame of my assignment doesn't allow for much subtlety.

So it is first period on Wednesday when I enter Sam's AP European History class. I come in two minutes before the bell. Late enough not to be early. Early enough not to be late.

A few pairs of eyes rise upon my entrance. I am acknowledged and dismissed.

Exactly what I want.

I sit in the back row and I wait.

Sam comes in.

She is tall and athletic, the hardness of her body contrasted by the soft curls that spill down her cheeks and pool around her shoulders.

The photos did not do her justice. She is stunning.

She enters with confidence and sits near the front of the room. She is surrounded by friends, a beautiful girl with black hair to her right, a huge boy with a sloppy shag cut to her left. This Shaggy Giant is making a great effort to look casual.

The door swings open and the teacher comes in, a thin man with a beard, time pulling on the corners of his eyes. His face betrays his age, but his energy does not. In most schools teachers are tired, but not here. Here they are passionate.

This teacher enters the room in midlecture, as if he can't wait to begin, so much so that he started his lecture in the hall outside class. Hell, he probably started in the parking lot this morning.

"Roosevelt and the Lend-Lease Act," he says.

The class goes silent. He glances at me briefly. His brain has registered a discrepancy. I see it on his face.

He looks down at his roster, finds my name.

"New," he says.

"Lucky me," I say.

A few kids chuckle.

"Welcome. We'll get you up to speed quickly," he says, and he dives back into his lecture. "America lends arms to Britain during World War Two, ending American neutrality without officially entering the war. Tell me, was it an act of cowardice or simply good diplomacy?"

I know this question. I know where it is near the end of the AP European syllabus. Unit ten. The Rise of Dictators and World War II.

I know the entire high school syllabus. I've studied all of it; it's just a matter of brushing up enough to remember these particular lessons.

If I wanted to, I could jump into the debate, fight my way to the top of the intellectual heap. But it would not serve me. Today I will hang back, listen, and learn.

And watch.

It seems I'm not the only one.

Sam monitors the debate, or what passes for a debate with this group. It's more like a discussion of the motivation behind U.S. diplomatic initiatives. At least until Sam jumps in.

"We should have been involved in the war years before we were," she says. "The Lend-Lease Act was passed by a single vote in Congress. Nobody wanted to be involved. We refused to choose a side."

"Wait a minute," a guy who looks like a soccer player says. "It wasn't our war at the time. Hitler invaded Poland, not Pittsburgh."

"So if it doesn't happen here, it's none of our business, right, Justin? Out of sight, out of mind. Like Darfur. Like Sarajevo."

"What about Iraq? We got involved there," another girl says.

"Economic interests," Sam says. "I'm talking about doing the right thing for the right reasons."

"You want the U.S. to make policy decisions based on morality?" Justin says. "That's not the real world. In the real world, things are complicated. Just ask your father."

"What do you mean by that?" Sam says, her back stiffening.

"Your father is sweeping up the homeless and warehousing them out of state. Is that the right thing?"

"Out of bounds," the teacher says. "Remember our ground rules. Unless Mayor Goldberg was in office in the 1940s, he's not part of this discussion."

"Wait," Sam says. "I want to talk about it. Because that's not what's happening. My father would never do that."

"Reality called," Justin says. "It says it misses you."

"I'm sick of this," Sam says.

She slams her book down on her desk.

"I'm sick of the bullshit intellectualism that passes for debate in this school." She jumps up. "We think we're so smart sitting here and arguing for hours, meanwhile people are suffering around the world, and our government refuses to take sides. And what do we do to change that? Talk and talk some more."

"What are you doing about it?" Justin says.

Sam doesn't say anything.

"So you're just like us," Justin says. "All talk."

Sam stands with fists clenched, her face blotched red.

"He's full of it," the Shaggy Giant says. He puts a hand on her arm.

"Let go of me!" she says. "I'm fine."

But she's not fine. Her eyes are darting around like she's going to hurt someone.

It's a big reaction to a little class debate. And it's got me wondering about Sam's emotional stability.

Most of the class look away from her, staring at their desks or scribbling in notebooks.

Sam takes a minute to calm herself.

"I'm sorry," she says, and she sits back down.

"It's okay," her friend with black hair says. She rubs Sam's back.

"It's just politics," Justin says. "Nothing personal."

"For me, politics *is* personal," Sam says.

The teacher purses his lips, looks back and forth between the students.

"Now would be a good time to lighten the mood with a joke," he says. "But my sense of humor seems to have left the building."

The students laugh. The mood is broken.

I see Sam's frustration as she attempts to disengage from the debate.

Passion plus intellect, with some deep emotional baggage beneath the surface.

It's an unusual combination. Challenging.

The question remains: How do I approach her?

I don't have the answer yet. But I'm getting closer.

The teacher says, "Ladies and gentlemen, your mission, should you choose to accept it—"

I'm expecting a groan, but I get the opposite. Excited faces, notebooks open, pens at the ready.

"Our dramatis personae: Stalin, Hitler, Mussolini," the teacher says.

He scans the room, a mischievous grin on his face. He glances at me and moves on.

"The scenario: These three infamous dictators meet in hell to discuss their mistakes during the war. Write it in the form of a dialogue, ten pages minimum. You may work with a partner."

The end-of-class tone sounds, and the students stand, looking to partner up and talk about the assignment.

I'm packing my backpack when I hear Sam's voice:

"What about you, new guy? Which side are you on?"

She's standing over my desk staring down at me. No posse now. Just her, a couple of feet away and glaring.

First contact. And I didn't choose it.

I can think about why she's here later. Now I have to react.

"You really want to know what the new guy thinks?" I say.

"You're the only one who didn't say a word all class, and I was the only one who actually cared about it, so yeah, I'd like to know," Sam says.

"Maybe the new guy is stupid and doesn't have much to say."

"Doubtful."

I want to shake her up if I can, try to regain the upper hand. So I say, "I think the assignment is bullshit."

She nods, interested. "Go on," she says.

"Why should we assume the dictators are in hell?"

"Hitler doesn't belong in hell. Is that what you're saying?"

"No. I'm saying the underlying assumption of the assignment has gone unchallenged. Dictators are bad. War is bad. Bad people go to hell and good people go to heaven. It's simplistic."

"So you're making a case for moral relativism."

"Why not?" I say, and I see her bristle. "Every dictator on the list believed he was right at the time. Or at minimum, he was doing wrong for the right reasons."

"The ends justify the means."

"Sometimes they do. It's easy to be outraged about genocide

because what's the counterargument? It doesn't exist. But think about a whistle-blower at a company. A father who cheats on his taxes to have enough money to pay his child's tuition. A mother who lies about her medical history to get health insurance."

And me.

The things I do. My assignments.

"All bad things," I say. "All good reasons."

"So I can hurt someone if it will be for the greater good?" Sam asks.

"Maybe so."

"The problem with that is—who gets to decide what the greater good is?"

"That's a fair question," I say.

"Do you have an answer?"

Who gets to decide?

I think about it for a second.

"Not us," I say.

She crosses her arms and gives me a disappointed head shake.

"Sounds like the new guy is a Republican," Sam says. "I'll have fun crushing you in future debates."

She smirks at me, then turns and walks away.

Conversation over. For now.

THE SHAGGY GIANT IS WAITING FOR ME OUTSIDE.

The moment I'm out the door, he steps up to block my path.

"Did you really get kicked out of Choate?" he says.

News travels fast in this school.

I look at this guy playing alpha, his chest out, his tone mocking. I consider the options, and I decide to answer the question, see what he's up to.

"I really got kicked out," I say.

"For being an asshole?"

"A big one."

"That's not going to fly here."

Behind him, Sam is talking to a girl with blond hair, a skin-tight skirt, and dimples. Not someone from AP European. Edgier than her other friends. I watch their body language as they speak.

The Shaggy Giant notices my attention has drifted from him. "You get distracted easily."

I look back at him.

This guy talks a good game. It's time to push back a little, see how good he really is.

"I'm not distracted," I say. "You had nothing interesting to say, so I assumed the conversation was over."

"I'll tell you when it's over."

"Who are you, my mother?"

"I'm your worst nightmare, my friend. I'm the guy between you and what you want."

He points at me. One long finger stabbing in the air.

"What do I want?"

"Every new guy in school makes a play for Sam," he says. "It's the fastest way to get in."

That explains it. He's got some connection to Sam.

"I'm not making a play," I say.

"I saw you talking to her after class."

"She was talking to me."

"In your dreams," he says.

"Believe what you want to believe."

He frowns, glances behind him. Sam and her group head down the hall without him, disappearing from view.

"I guess Sam's your girlfriend?" I say.

He twitches.

Guess not.

"For your information, we are longtime friends," he says. "I look out for her. Think of me as the early asshole warning system."

"You specialize in ass, that's what you're telling me."

"Funny man," he says. "Consider yourself warned."

He points at me again.

I AM THE WEAPON

Less than a second, I think. That's the amount of time it would take to disable him.

A quick grab and twist. In the movies the tough guy pulls the finger backward toward the wrist. That's effective enough, but it takes a little too long.

The finger joint has backward flexibility, but very little side flex. If it's about speed and shock, a side snap works better.

Shaggy Giant stands with his finger outstretched, not realizing the danger he's in. But I don't need to take this guy down, not yet at least. Better to show him I'm not afraid and use his anger to find out more about Sam in the coming days.

He says, "I'm watching you. Don't forget that."

"How could I forget?" I say. "You're fourteen feet tall."

I USE MY LUNCH HOUR TO GO TO THE APPLE STORE.

That's the benefit of an open campus. I leave school without causing so much as a head turn and walk south, taking the opportunity to learn the neighborhood better.

The best way to do that is to walk. Walk and walk some more. Walk until I feel like a local.

As I walk, I think about Sam. Why she might have approached me in class.

I don't know her well enough yet, so I table the question for now.

When I get to the gleaming glass cube on 67th Street, I walk in and buy the newest iPhone with cash.

"Do you want me to set it up for you?" the guy at the Genius Bar says.

"You're the genius," I say.

He nods appreciatively.

"You'd be surprised how few people get that," he says.

74

He turns it toward me, and I type in my Apple ID for this assignment.

He gets the phone set up and hands it back to me.

"How's your Wi-Fi here?" I say.

"It's awesome."

"Maybe I'll download some apps before I go."

"Let it rip."

I find a corner of a table to lean on, go to the App Store on my phone. I search for an app called High School Locker. I download it and open it up. A graphic of a combination lock appears on my screen.

Type in a combination! Keep pics, videos, and books in your very own locker, away from prying eyes!

I put in a combination code. Not a three-number code like a person using the app. I put in a ten-digit code. When I finish, there's a click, and the lock starts to spin.

A progress bar appears on the bottom of the screen.

The phone is handshaking with a secret server, downloading a sophisticated security suite, and installing it.

The lock stops spinning and the phone restarts.

It looks the same, but the phone is now jail-broken. Two operating systems are running. One on the surface, one beneath.

Slide the bar to the right, and the phone is in public mode. If someone found it, they'd see a regular iPhone. They could make calls, play games, whatever.

But if I use the unique diagonal finger gesture, it's in secure mode. Now I've got access to an entire suite of apps that make this phone very special.

I put it in secure mode now, then open the camera. I configure the settings, triple-clicking the flash. I hold it up to take a picture—

"Hey, is that the new iPhone?" a girl says.

She's maybe fifteen, long brown hair, too much gloss on her lips. She has a backpack slung across one shoulder. The strap pulls her shirt tight, the swell of her breast pressing against fabric.

"Brand-new," I say.

"I wish I could afford one." Her eyes widen. "Do you want me to take a picture of you?"

"I do," I say.

I hand her the phone.

"It's beautiful," she says.

"Me or the phone?"

"Definitely the phone," she says. But she's laughing as she says it.

"It's all set up," I say. "Just press the button."

She takes my photo. It's not really a photo, but she doesn't know that.

She just sent a locator ping back to Father.

I am here. I have begun.

I reach out to take the phone back.

There's a man across the store looking at us. Curly hair and a tightly shaved beard. Dark complexion, intense eyes.

Too intense.

He might be looking at us, but I can't be certain. By the time I look in his direction, he has turned away. Not in reaction to me, at least it seems not, but as part of a sweep around the room.

I watch him for a moment. He's in his early twenties, short with a wiry build. Maybe a gym rat, maybe something else. Something that requires a different kind of training.

"Do you have a boyfriend?" I ask the girl.

That might explain the guy with the beard.

"Not at the moment," the girl says. She smiles, misunderstanding why I asked the question. "Hey, should we take a picture together? Capture the moment and all that?"

She applies a little more gloss to her lips. They glimmer in the light of a laptop screen.

I glance back toward the man, but he's gone.

"Thanks," I say to the girl, "but I have to get back to school."

I take the phone from her.

"Where do you go?" she says.

I shrug and mumble something as I walk away, blowing her off.

She looks disappointed.

No matter. I have work to do.

I STEP OUT OF THE STORE AND I FEEL IT IMMEDIATELY.

A presence.

Following me.

It's on the very edge of my awareness. Nearly imperceptible.

Is it the Shaggy Giant?

Doubtful.

The man with the beard in the Apple Store?

Possibly.

I stand in place, projecting the circle of my attention in all directions like sonar.

I take a step. I listen.

I detect no movement, no disturbance.

So I walk north, heading back toward school. I stop at the intersection of Broadway and Amsterdam. I wait at the light, using the time to scan in all directions.

Still nothing.

My training has taught me to trust my intuition, but also to test it.

That's what I do now.

I nod to a security guard smoking a cigarette in a drugstore doorway, use the pause to break my rhythm. At the corner of 72nd, I take a sudden turn toward West End Avenue, where it's less crowded, and more difficult to track someone undetected.

That's when I feel it again.

The Presence. He's a man.

It's not the Shaggy Giant. He would be too close, pressuring me.

The Presence is skilled. Maybe he's part of the mayor's security detail.

I replay the conversation with Sam earlier. I consider briefly the idea that something is going on in her life sufficient to have her worried about a new guy, worried enough to have him checked out by security.

I consider, then I dismiss it. I haven't done anything in this city.

Not yet, at least.

But the Presence is here nonetheless. He turns as I turn, staying parallel to me, a block east on Broadway.

I have a choice: Lose him or flush him out?

I could lose him temporarily. Slip into a building, hop a cab, double back.

I could lose him permanently. Lead him into Riverside Park. Overpower him and ask a few questions. Leave his body for an early-morning jogger to discover.

But I don't want added police attention in the neighborhood this week.

It's better to flush him now and find out who he is.

Whether he's related to Sam, to The Program, or to nothing at all. I need to know.

I speed up and head back toward school. I sense him continuing along with me on Broadway. I remember a church I saw earlier on my walk through the neighborhood. A church with an alley next door.

I can use it.

I walk east on 81st, projecting my energy toward Broadway as if I'm going to appear there, but I cut through the alley instead, pop out at the church on 80th, and double back.

If I've timed it right, I'll catch the Presence on 81st. A quiet street. Light traffic.

No place to hide.

I wait two more seconds, then I step out into the street at the corner of 81st and West End, look back toward Broadway.

There's nobody there.

The tiniest flicker of doubt crosses my mind. Am I imagining this?

I breathe slowly, project my energy into the circle around me, expanding it outward by degrees.

Nothing.

Whoever he is, he's good.

And he's gone.

I'VE GOT MY NEW PHONE IN HAND.

It's time to use it.

I slip into the lobby of a large building and find a quiet corner. I use the special finger gesture to put the phone into secure mode, then I look up *Dad* in the contacts.

It's a number I haven't seen before.

If I press the number, it will brick the phone, effectively destroying it.

So I don't touch it. Instead I go to the picture box at the top of the contact information. A *World's Greatest Dad* T-shirt. I pull the photo to the right, and the name *Dad* disappears, replaced with a new phone number.

I press the number.

"It's me," I say.

"I got the photo you sent earlier," Father says. "Looks like you're off and running."

"Yes and no," I say.

Silence on the line. I've deviated from protocol, and Father instantly recognizes it.

"Is there a problem?" he says.

What's the best way to ask him about the Presence?

I decide to test a hypothesis. What if the Presence was sent from The Program to monitor me?

It's never happened before, at least not to my knowledge. I've been on the road for two years now, receiving assignments and being left alone to carry them out.

But this assignment is something different. An accelerated timeline and a target with a high profile, maybe the highest profile of anyone in the city. It's at least possible that I'm being monitored more closely.

So I say, "I'm wondering if I saw someone you might know."

"I don't know many people in New York," he says cautiously.

"Maybe it was a friend you sent to check up on me? Since I'm new here and all."

"Where did you see this person?" Father says.

Tension seizes his voice. He covers it well. There is perhaps a 5 percent elevation in pitch.

A normal person would not hear it.

But I can.

"I didn't see him exactly," I say. "It was more of a casual thing. At the Apple Store and again on the street just now."

"Did you speak with him?" Father says.

"It wasn't a speaking situation."

It was a following situation. I walked, and he followed me.

"I don't know anything about it," Father says.

I listen to his voice, trying to judge whether he's telling the truth. It sounds like he is. Which would mean the Presence is not related to The Program. But I can't say for sure.

"I hope he didn't bother you," Father says.

"He didn't."

"This conversation has me concerned. Especially given the timeline of your new assignment."

"Yes, it's a tight one," I say.

"You can't afford any distractions. Your mother and I were talking about what happened the last time."

"What are you referring to?"

"The four obstacles."

He's talking about the Chinese spies.

"Mother told me it was no big deal," I say.

"In and of itself, no. But I don't want to think there's a pattern here. Unexpected things popping up suddenly."

A pattern of what? Is Father suggesting that I've screwed up?

"I'm sure it was nothing," I say.

Back to business. Back to being in control.

I say, "I'm not even convinced I saw anything. I just thought I should check with you."

"I'm glad you did—something important like this."

"I have to go now," I say. "I have to get back to school."

"Of course. Keep me in the loop," he says. "And if you see this person again, let me know."

"I will."

The line disconnects.

I'm troubled by this conversation with Father and the questions it raises.

But there's nothing I can do about it now.

I scan the lobby, looking for anything out of place. I don't find it. Only people in business suits gliding up and down the escalators, going about their day.

It's time for me to go on with mine.

A CRY ECHOES DOWN THE SCHOOL CORRIDOR.

I'm walking in the hall after sixth period when I hear it.

"Cut it out!" a high-pitched voice says.

It sounds like a girl.

It's not.

It's the pale kid from the cluster group this morning.

He's down the far end of the hall, pushed into a nearly invisible cubbyhole off the main hallway.

This school has a lot of unique study areas. L-shapes, dead ends, mini cul-de-sacs. Nooks and crannies laid out with beanbag chairs, most with large windows looking out on the New York skyline. If this were a prison, these would be considered traps. Blind spots the guards cannot monitor and where anything could happen. Here they are not traps but alternative study environments.

Hence the two guys teaching this boy a lesson by beating the crap out of him.

"Stop it!" Pale says.

I hear cursing, and a *thump*. The bigger of the two guys straight-arms him into the wall. It's Justin, the guy with the soccer build from the AP class. A serious jock. He hits the geeky kid like a freight train while his buddy with a greasy face looks on.

The kid takes his punishment, his body limp, arms flopping at his sides. He doesn't even hold his hands up in front of himself. No defense at all. They've beaten it out of him.

The application of might. It's the same all over the world.

But it has nothing to do with me or my assignment, so I continue down the hall, minding my own business but monitoring the action in my peripheral vision.

As I pass by, Justin punches the geek in the stomach. It's more of a half punch, crooked elbow, no backswing. But still, it's a punch in the guts.

Ruthless.

I could stop this in a second. Clear my throat. Cast some attention in their direction.

I could stop it in other ways, too. I could make sure it never happens again. I could make sure Justin never raises his arm above waist level. No more throwing or catching or whatever the hell he does to get laid after school. I could remove his arm altogether.

But that wouldn't serve my assignment.

The pale kid grunts in pain, and I ignore it and keep walking.

Uninvolved. That's the best way to play it.

Or so I think until I hear a girl's voice behind me.

Sam's voice.

"Cut the shit!" she says.

I turn back to find her standing outside the cubbyhole, her arms crossed hard over her chest.

Involved. That's how she plays it. Of course.

Her timing is lousy. I've blown my chance to grandstand in front of her. Now I'll have to play catch-up.

"Mind your own business," the jock says to her.

"I'm making it my business, Justin," Sam says.

Justin steps out of the cubbyhole, confronts her face-to-face. He's towering over her. He's got eight inches and ninety pounds on her.

She doesn't care. She stands her ground.

Impressive.

Justin says, "What are you going to do, Sam? Run to your daddy crying?"

He says her name with a sneer, adding syllables where none exist.

It's time to get back into this thing. The casual hero. That's the way I'll play it.

I turn toward them, interested, but no more than any student passing by might be.

"What's going on?" I say.

I say it low and even-toned, not like I'm going to do anything about it, but like I'm a good citizen.

Justin looks up at me. He looks back at Sam. His greasy friend is by his side.

I take a step toward them.

Sam looks at me.

"We're out of here," Justin says.

He and his buddy walk down the hall in my direction.

I walk toward Sam, not diverting, but giving the guys room. As Justin passes by, he pulls back a fist like he's going to punch me in the face.

Our eyes meet briefly.

He puts his fist down.

When I get to Sam, she's pulling the pale kid up off the floor.

"You're all right, Howard," she says to him. She brushes dirt out of his hair. Her finger snags in the tangle.

He looks at the ground, mortified.

"Thanks, Sam," he says.

"Should I call someone?" she says. "Do you need the nurse?"

"I'm fine," he says, embarrassed. He pulls away from her, rushing away down the hall.

Sam sighs and watches him go.

"Everything okay here?" I say.

I keep it low-key. I don't brag.

I saved the day, and it's no big deal to me. That's what I want to communicate.

"No thanks to you," Sam says.

"Hey, I stepped up," I say.

"What are you talking about? I saw you walk right past him. No surprise from the guy who doesn't believe in right and wrong."

Bad news. She saw me, and the hero act is not going to work.

My fallback position?

Play the rebel. *I'm caught and I don't care.*

I say, "I'm the new guy, remember? I mind my own business."

"History is filled with guys like you. They're the ones who stand by while the war crimes happen."

"You don't know me," I say.

"I don't want to know you," she says, and she brushes past.

I watch her huff her way down the hall.

Not good. First day and I'm already on her shit list. If I had more time, I'd say it was an achievement to get on the radar in any way.

But with my timeline, I have to find a way to turn this around fast.

"She has issues with men," a voice says.

It's the pale kid, Howard. He's been hiding around the corner and listening.

"What kind of issues?" I say.

"She had her heart broken."

"Really?"

"A few years ago. She had a superserious boyfriend who messed with her head."

I need to hear that story, but I put it aside for a moment, focus instead on Howard. On the fact that he knows this about Sam.

A boy without options, adopted by the one girl who will give him the time of day. And she happens to be at the top of the pyramid.

Howard is on the inside. If need be, I can use this fact.

"Should I go after her?" I say.

I say it like someone who is unsure, who needs help with girls from someone like Howard.

"It depends what you want," he says.

"What could I want?"

"To break her heart."

"I don't do that," I say. "It's not my style."

"You're right," he says. "She'll probably break yours."

I laugh. *Nothing to worry about there, Howard.*

He looks at me, deciding.

"If it were me, I would go after her," he says.

Why isn't it you? That's what I'm thinking. But I'll leave that question for another time.

"Be gentle," he says. "She's famous, but she's still a person."

"Thanks for the advice," I say.

"My name is Howard," he says.

"I owe you one, Howard."

"DO YOU HAVE A THREE-STRIKES POLICY?" I SAY TO SAM.

She ignores me and keeps walking. I follow a few paces behind. Not rushing. But also not afraid.

"Why do you ask?" she says over her shoulder.

"Because I was an asshole in class and then I walked away from a fight. I figure I'm at two and I need to know how careful I should be right now."

"Bad news," she says. "I'm a two-strikes kind of girl."

"So I've blown it."

"Big-time," she says. "But what do you care?"

Because I need to get close to your father.

"I don't know," I say. "For some reason I do. Something about you, I guess. I can see you're different."

It's a classic ploy. Express interest in a girl you just met. If you do it right, you can charm her, or at least pique her interest.

"You're playing games," she says. "We don't know each other, so how do you know I'm different?"

So much for the classics.

If one path doesn't work, try another. That's what I've been taught.

I played the rebel earlier in the hall. Now I'll be the rebel who has seen the light. What would that guy say in this situation?

"Maybe I feel guilty," I say. "Maybe you woke me up a little with what you said about me being a bystander."

She considers this.

"Have you ever seen a little kid ice-skating for the first time?" she says.

"Change of subject, huh?"

"Have you?"

Genesee Valley Park.

The name pops into my head. A place I haven't thought about in years. I remember learning to skate there when I was a kid, my father walking backward in front of me, his arms outstretched, urging me to come toward him.

I don't want to be remembering this.

I pull myself back to the moment. Sam in front of me. Her question.

"I've seen kids skate," I say.

"Inevitably a kid is going to slip on the ice, and his body will contort into all kinds of crazy positions as he tries to steady himself. He'll do anything not to fall down."

"Your point is?"

"That's you," she says. "Right now. You'll say anything, won't you?"

This girl is like a human lie detector. I stand there, stalling for time, trying to find the next mode of attack.

"Even now," she says, "you're trying to think of the right thing to say to me."

I feel my face flush. I never react like this. Not to a girl. Not to anyone.

Follow her lead, I think. *Go with it and don't lie.*

"You're right. I'll say anything right now."

"Why?"

"I want to meet you."

"Finally, the truth," she says.

"A lot of girls prefer if guys lie. As long as they're hearing what they want to hear."

"I'm not a lot of girls."

"I'm starting to see that."

She looks at me. Not really a look. More like an MRI.

"I'm Samara," she says, and she extends her hand.

I reach for it. Her hand is soft and warm, much warmer than I expected it to be.

"I know who you are," I say.

"I guess everyone knows."

"They only know your reputation."

She sighs.

"Thanks for putting it that way. Not many people get that."

"I get it."

"Maybe *you're* the one who's different," she says.

"You'll say anything right now, won't you?" I say.

She smiles.

"You're using my own lines against me?" she says.

"All's fair in love and war."

"Which one are we doing, new guy?"

I look at her eyes, a beautiful smoky gray flecked with green.

Suddenly I am somewhere else, standing in front of someone else....

A GIRL.

The first one. Not like Sam. This girl had long blond hair and blue eyes.

I was fourteen at the time. The girl was older. Seventeen or eighteen.

She was a cashier in a convenience store. I met her one day when Father took me out to do errands with him. It was my second year of training and things were different. Mother and Father trusted me. I even got to leave the house sometimes.

The cashier smiled and slipped me a note. It said we should meet.

I thought that something real was happening between us. Maybe I wanted to feel what it was like to be normal, just once. A normal guy hooking up with a beautiful girl.

We met at her house later that night. She walked me straight through the house and didn't stop until we got to her bedroom.

She closed the door behind her.

And then she started to unbutton her blouse.

I remember a red bra. Nipples visible through lace.

"Do you like me?" she said.

"Of course," I said. She seemed to be okay with that answer because she kept unbuttoning.

She paused at the bottom button. She bit her lip like something was troubling her.

"You're very young," she said.

"Not so young," I said.

She put a hand on my shoulder. "Here's the thing," she said. "You're going to think you love me after this."

I'd had nearly two years of training at the time. I'd become tough in a way I did not know was possible.

When she mentioned love, I shook my head no.

She took my face in her hands. I remember how warm her skin felt against mine.

"Trust me on this," she said. "You're going to think you love me. And you're going to think I love you because I gave you my body."

She let her blouse drop to the floor.

"You'll be wrong about both things," she said.

BUT THAT WAS A LONG TIME AGO.

I shouldn't be thinking about it. Not now.

Now it is Sam who is standing in front of me, waiting for an answer.

All's fair in love and war, I said.

Which one are we doing? she asked.

"I don't know which one," I say. "But I'd like to find out."

"Fair enough," she says. "Maybe we could start with you telling me your name."

My name.

My real name is somewhere near the back of my brain, swept into a far corner, where it's out of sight. I've got a pile of things back there. Names, images, moments, memories.

The artifacts of a former life. None of them useful to me now.

"My name is Benjamin," I say.

My name for now. My name for this assignment. My name for her.

"Benjamin," she says. "An old man's name."

"I've got an old soul."

She studies my face.

"We're similar that way," she says.

The class tone sounds.

"I apologize if I put you on the spot before, Benjamin. I have to be really careful because of my father. A lot of people want to know me for the wrong reasons."

"You threw me for a second. I'm not used to someone being so honest."

"I think it's good for you," she says.

A second tone sounds. The hallway fills with people.

"Nice to meet you, Sam."

I turn away, heading for my next class.

"There's a party tonight," she says.

I stop.

"You should come by. We do it every April Fool's, and it's my turn to host this year."

"At the mayor's residence?" I say.

"Also known as my apartment."

Her father doesn't live in Gracie Mansion. He prefers his double apartment on the Upper West Side. It's more private, and because of that, it's a more exclusive invite. One I'm not in a position to turn down.

"A party sounds nice," I say.

The final class tone sounds.

"Good. Then I'll see you later," Sam says.

She smiles.

I'm in.

To show up at Sam's party alone would be death. Wander in as the new guy with the pity invite, then spend the night nursing Diet Cokes while leaning on walls and making small talk. I could turn it around quickly once I was there, but it would be a lot of work.

There are better ways.

The best would be to skip the party altogether, let Sam wonder why I blew her off, chase me, allow the mystery to grow.

But that takes time, and time is what I don't have.

I need to find another option.

I'm walking through school thinking about it when I turn a corner and see a girl studying in a beanbag chair. It's the blond who was talking with Sam this morning. The one in the skintight skirt.

Well, half a skirt.

She's flopped out on a beanbag, fighting her way through a chemistry textbook. She reads a little, then sighs, then reads.

I may have just found a better way to go to Sam's party. I make a U-turn and head for her.

"Is this bean taken?" I say.

She glances up from her reading.

"Free," she says, and goes back to the book.

I plop down. I take out a math book and bury myself in it, ignoring her.

I wait.

Ninety seconds later she glances over.

I wait.

She glances again. That's my opening. "What's up in the world of chem?" I say.

"It's making my brain hurt," she says.

She looks like a lot of things make her brain hurt. But I keep the thought to myself.

"Chem is painful," I say. "But it's nothing compared to trig."

I hold up the math book.

"I ruptured a blood vessel in my head twenty minutes ago," I say, "but we were two chapters behind in my last school, so I can't stop until I catch up."

"Wouldn't you be paralyzed from a rupture?" she says.

"I am. But it's only my left side."

I flop my left hand around like it's dead.

She laughs. This girl has a sense of humor. Maybe she isn't so bad after all.

"So you're new?" she says.

"Sucks, huh?"

"High likelihood of sucking," she says.

She closes her book and flips it onto her lap. I close my book, too.

"I'm pretty good with that chem stuff," I say. "If there's anything I can do."

She bites her lower lip.

"What do you know about chemical reactions?"

"Plenty," I say, and I wink.

Corny, I know. Sam would probably snap my neck if I said something like that to her, but this girl is just the type who might like it.

"That is so cheesy," the girl says, and makes a sour face.

She likes it.

"What's your name?" she says.

"Benjamin," I say.

"Can I call you Benji?"

"If you do, I'll never talk to you again."

"How about Ben?" she says.

"Why do you care what you call me?"

"I want to know what I should put in my phone when I type in your number."

"I didn't give you my number," I say.

"Not yet," she says. "But you want to."

She's right about that.

She sighs and stretches long and slow as she lies back on the beanbag chair. I make sure to look at her bare legs, just like a horny sixteen-year-old would. She's got nice legs.

"I just got a new phone," I say.

"Perfect," she says.

I give her my number.

Her name is Erica. That's what I find out.

By the end of the day we've shot a dozen funny text messages back and forth, and Erica and I have made plans to go to Sam's party together.

She even believes it's her idea.

I HAVE AN APARTMENT IN THE CITY.

An apartment I've never seen.

The address is uptown on 98th Street. When I leave school, I head there, winding my way through the West Side.

I look at the neighborhood in a different way now. The illusion of my invisibility has been shattered.

The Presence is on my mind.

I make myself move like a distracted guy walking home after school, thinking about whatever normal high school guys think about. But in fact my attention is split. I watch store windows for trails. I monitor the faces of people on the street, checking their expressions for the tell that accompanies recognition. Taxis and delivery trucks are no longer neutral to me because I know the things that are most ubiquitous in the environment are the things most easily used against me.

I use all my skills to monitor my journey north, but I find nothing.

No tail. No danger. No Presence.

Eventually I'm standing alone in front of a decent walk-up building on 98th between Broadway and West End Avenue.

I let the questions about the Presence go, and I focus on the building.

No doorman. Nobody to watch me.

The street is a little north of the expensive area where most students live, but still affluent enough to be believable for a guy in private school, a guy whose parents wanted more space, maybe needed to find a little bit of a bargain.

I remove a well-worn key from my pocket. It slides easily into the front door lock, despite my never having used it before.

I take the stairs to the second floor. I have a bag from Lenny's Bagels swinging on my arm and a backpack on my shoulder. If anyone should see me, I am just a new guy who moved in a little while ago, coming home late from school.

I use another key in the door of the apartment. The door swings open, creaking slightly on its hinges.

The odor hits me. Not unpleasant. A different kind of smell.

Lived-in.

This apartment where I have never lived smells lived-in.

In fact, it smells like someone's home.

I walk into the apartment and turn on a light.

It is not a large apartment. Two bedrooms. A good-sized place by New York standards. Small by suburban standards.

I go into the smaller bedroom. My bedroom. Kids always have the smaller bedroom. This is what I've been told. Sure enough, my clothes are there, some in drawers, some scattered across the floor as if I've thrown them there.

I sit at the desk and open the top drawer.

It is filled with stationery supplies. I reach in and up, tapping the inside compartment of the drawer.

There is a pencil case there.

I carefully remove it.

I unzip the case.

Two mechanical pencils. A clickable pen. A pencil-shaped eraser with the brown paper that spirals from it in long strips.

On the desk is a watch. An empty iPhone charging cradle waits beside it.

My tools.

I tap the phone from the Apple Store, and it comes to life. I use the finger gestures that put it in secure mode.

I call Father.

He was concerned earlier. I want to give him a progress update that will put him at ease.

"Nice to hear from you again," he says. "And so soon."

I hear the question in his voice.

"I met a new friend," I say.

"A new friend? That's wonderful."

"I think you'd like her."

I'm speaking in code, telling Father that I've connected with my mark.

"One day in a new school and you already have a friend," Father says. "That's very good."

I imagine him telling Mother the news, the two of them talking about what a good job I'm doing on this assignment. The thought pleases me.

"My new friend invited me to a party tonight," I say.

I walk into the master bedroom as I talk. A smiling couple stares out at me from the picture on the bedside table. I pick up the photo and look at the strangers standing arm in arm.

My parents. Supposedly.

In fact I've never seen these people before. The photos have been staged here in the event someone should have to enter the apartment. I memorize the faces in case I need to describe them in the future.

I look at other photos in which they appear. One in particular gets my attention. It's a photo of these people at the beach. The parents I've never seen relax on lounge chairs while a younger version of me relaxes beside them, digitally inserted into the frame.

"The party is at her dad's place," I say to Father.

"And it's tonight?" he says.

"I work fast," I say. Then I laugh like a cocky kid might.

"The acorn doesn't fall far from the tree," Father says. He laughs, too.

"My transition is going well. That's what I wanted you to know."

"Glad to hear it. And by the way, the thing we discussed earlier?"

"The thing?"

"The person you thought you saw. I ran it by your mother."

I stop moving, all my attention focused on the conversation. If he shared it with Mother, he's concerned.

And he never gets concerned.

"What did Mother say?"

"She said to be careful."

I'm always careful.

What does she mean?

"You're in a new city," Father says. "You don't know who to trust yet. There may be factors here with which you're not familiar."

"Because the assignment is so unusual?" I say.

"Unusual? Why do you use that word?"

It's a political assassination.

"The scale is different," I say. "The size. The timeline."

"It sounds like a good test of your skills," Father says.

A test.

Is that what it is?

IT WAS A BEAUTIFUL FALL DAY WHEN THEY BROUGHT ME TO THE TOWN.

The leaves were changing on the trees, brilliant colors dappled across the landscape. I watched them flash by as we drove away from our training house.

Mother and Father sat in the front seat, and I was in the back. A family out for a Sunday drive. That's what you might have thought had you passed by us.

Mother said I'd earned some downtime. I'd been working hard, she said, and it was high time that I enjoyed myself.

She stopped the car near a small town.

"We'll see you later," she said.

"Later?"

Father palmed me some money, five crisp twenty-dollar bills folded in half.

"What do I do with this?" I said.

"See a movie. Have lunch. Enjoy yourself."

"How will I get back?"

"Taken care of," Father said.

His voice sounded strange. It was strained in a way I didn't recognize then. I almost asked him about it, but when I looked out the window, people were walking down the main street of a small town where everything was decorated for Halloween.

I didn't ask Father what was wrong. I got out of the car instead.

It was the first time I'd been alone and on my own in nearly two years.

I walked through town. Pumpkins, cutouts of ghosts, black-and-orange wreaths hanging in store windows.

I waited for the car to come back, but it did not.

"Is there a movie theater?" I asked a middle-aged woman.

There was a new action movie playing, and I wanted to see it. Badly.

"Six blocks down around the corner," she said. "Only one screen."

"I only need one."

She pointed down and to the right.

I sucked in cool fall air. Where was I?

The Northeast? New Hampshire or Vermont?

Or was I farther south, someplace like rural Maryland?

I wanted to ask her, but I didn't want to draw attention to myself. To ask directions to a local theater is one thing. To ask what state you're in is something else.

I walked. I breathed. Leaves crunched beneath my feet.

I felt lucky. My new parents trusted me. The Program trusted me.

I had proved myself. I was one of them and worthy of this trust.

The devil smiled at me from inside a hardware store. I smiled back.

Freedom, if just for an afternoon.

That's when I felt it.

Someone was following me through town. After a minute, one person became several people. And then the whole world went mad.

I didn't know that it was my graduation day, and by the end there would be only two people standing.

I was one. Mike was the other.

It was the day of the great fight.

It was the day of the knife.

I never did see that movie. I was too busy fighting for my life.

ANOTHER TEST.

That's what this assignment is.

"Are you there?" Father says on the phone.

"I'm here," I say. "I was thinking about something."

"Something you care to share with me?"

I take a long breath.

"You said there are factors I might not be familiar with this time."

"That's right."

"Maybe the factors won't matter," I say.

"What do you mean?"

"The party tonight. Maybe I'll be finished with my assignment before you know it, and I won't have to worry about any of these factors."

"That would make life simpler," Father says.

"Much simpler for everyone," I say.

ERICA SMIRKS WHEN SHE SEES ME.

She's sitting in the window of the bookstore at 82nd and Broadway, nursing a nearly empty cup of coffee.

I don't go inside, just nod to her. A minute later she comes bounding out the door, all smiles and breathiness.

"Hey, you," she says.

She hugs me too tightly, then pulls back quickly and touches her boob.

"Ouch. What poked me?" she says.

I reach into my jacket pocket, pull out the weaponized ballpoint I've brought with me for tonight.

"My lucky pen," I say.

"Why do you need a lucky pen?"

"I like it. My father gave it to me."

Not true. The Program gave it to me. But she'll never know that.

"You ready to head over?" I say.

"I changed my mind," she says. "Why don't we go to my place and watch a movie instead?"

I raise an eyebrow.

"April Fool's," she says.

"Cute."

"I know I am," she says.

Her cheeks flush red in the cool spring night. She is beautiful, looking at me with big, made-up eyes.

There is a sensation in my chest, a brief contraction like a muscle cramp.

Then it passes.

She takes my arm, hooking her elbow in mine as we walk.

"What's going on between you and Sam?" she says.

"What did she tell you?"

"*Nada*. But I've got women's intuition."

"There's nothing's going on," I say. "The new guy got a pity invite."

I feel her arm relax in mine.

"So I still have a chance?" she says.

Her comment exposes a lifetime of competition. I imagine being best friends with a girl who is rich, beautiful, and the mayor's daughter. No matter how bright you shine, there is always someone beside you, shining brighter.

I almost feel sorry for Erica.

"Does Sam have a boyfriend?" I say.

"Not for a while," Erica says.

"Any particular reason?"

"She had a superserious relationship with her ex. I don't think she's completely over it."

"Is he still around?" I say.

"No, it was always LD. I think that was half the problem. How do you have a relationship with someone who isn't here?"

I think about my father. I try to imagine what it would be like to talk to him today, the questions I would ask him, the things I'd tell him about my life since he's been gone.

"Long distance. Sounds painful," I say.

"Sometimes love hurts," she says.

"Sometimes?"

"If you're into spanking, it does. Hey, are we going to spend the whole night talking about Sam?"

She pulls my arm in tighter. I feel the swell of her breast against my elbow. It's not a bad feeling.

"It depends how fascinating you are," I say.

"I'm wildly fascinating," she says.

I LET ERICA GUIDE ME TO SAM'S APARTMENT.

It's on 81st between Central Park West and Columbus. Across from the Museum of Natural History.

I note the details outside:

There's a squad car parked at the end of the block. Another down the street on the opposite corner. There's a permanent police box installed out front on the sidewalk with room for one cop.

I note the details within:

A beautiful lobby, four men on duty at all times. A doorman, a concierge, an assistant, and the elevator operator. They're regulars. I can see by how relaxed they are. It's nearly impossible not to relax when you're in the same routine every day. You can drill, you can fight to maintain operational awareness, but day after day without incident wears down the attention. The brain cannot stay on high alert forever.

Danger focuses the mind.

No danger, no focus.

And with a bunch of students coming over for a party, there's no danger. Just a lot of young girls to look at.

When I walk in with Erica, I've got instant cred and a beautiful distraction by my side.

We flash IDs, and a guard with a clipboard checks off our names while looking down Erica's cleavage. Unprofessional, but useful. It means my face won't be remembered here.

An elevator operator takes us upstairs by tapping an electronic card to a sensor on the wall.

"That guy was an asshole," Erica whispers to me. "Did you see him looking down my dress?"

"It's hard not to look," I say to her.

She grins and pulls my arm closer.

"Coming from you, that's a compliment."

I glance at the elevator man. He makes sure to stare at the wall in front of him, expert at not hearing conversations a foot away from him.

"Mayor's residence," the elevator guy says.

The doors open into a short, custom-built hallway. An apartment like this would usually have an elevator that opens right into the living room or foyer. This hallway is an additional layer of security between the apartment and the world, and it speaks to the importance of the people who live here. No doubt this area can lock down from both sides, trapping you between the front door and the elevator door.

Good to know.

But we're not done quite yet.

There's another security detail to pass through. Two guys in dark suits who aren't cops, and clearly aren't temporary hires.

These guys are heavy hitters. I can tell the difference.

The first one is out of position, too close to the elevator. If something bad came through the elevator doors, he would be in trouble.

The second is situated better. He's across the hall with his back to a wall. He's in a good position to see what's going on. This one is not distracted. He scans faces, waistbands, hands. He's a real pro.

I'm impressed.

We pass by him and he nods to me. A nod, the universal greeting of military and law enforcement around the world when they recognize one of their own. He recognizes something in me, or his senses do. He's nodding to one of his own tribe.

I almost nod back.

It's so automatic that I barely catch it in time.

One nod and it would be over. If this guy is as good as I think he is, I'd have a lot of questions to answer.

So when he nods, I pretend not to notice. I instantly pull my energy back by a degree.

This Pro is dangerous. I will avoid him if I can.

His partner opens the doors for us. No nod.

Just the entrance to the mayor's residence on the penthouse floor.

I'm expecting the money shot from a New York billionaire. A grand room, the ceiling rising thirty feet in the air, a chandelier the size of a small car.

That's not what I see.

I see a home.

Natural tones. Shelves of books. Soft lighting.

Make no mistake. It's a huge space—the entire floor of a

building. But at the same time, it's comfortable. You can sense that real people live here. Some spaces are just like that.

Snacks.

The word pops into my head.

It disturbs me, the way it sneaks up on me and enters uninvited.

Kids come home and have snacks.

Why am I thinking about this? This is not real. It's something I saw on a TV show sometime.

No. It's a memory.

Twelve years old. My last year of normal life in the world.

My snack. Oatmeal raisin cookies on a plate.

"Earth to Benji," Erica says.

I look back at her. I can't afford the distraction of memories now, not when I've got five days to complete the highest-profile assignment of my life.

It could also be my quickest.

It all depends on the mayor. Is he here tonight?

"Sorry, I was thinking about something," I say to Erica.

"I know what you're thinking," she says. "You're thinking you're out of your league. That's what everyone thinks when they're in the mayor's house for the first time. Not cool, Ben. I need you *suavecito*."

"This place? What's the big deal?" I say.

"Exactly," she says. "That's the cocky guy I met this afternoon. Now follow me."

Music carries down the hall from another part of the apartment.

We walk toward it. The hall opens into a large living room. Music blares. Bodies jump.

Erica's energy turns excited, her shoulders swaying to the music.

"Isn't this great?" she shouts.

She dances in front of me, a single serpentine move, all hips and attitude.

I gauge the reactions of people around the room. Are they looking at us?

Yes. And they look surprised to see Erica with the new guy. But more importantly, will Sam be surprised?

"Where is she?" Erica is asking a girl. The girl points.

Erica turns her back to me, her ass swaying with the music. She glances back to see if I'm looking.

I am.

She guides me down the hall.

To Sam.

We catch up to her in a huge, state-of-the-art kitchen. Someone obviously likes to cook in this house, and it might be Sam. She's at the counter chopping vegetables with a large chef's knife.

"Look what I found," Erica says like she's showing me off.

Sam takes in the two of us standing together.

There's no obvious reaction, at least not that a normal person could detect.

But I'm not a normal person.

I see a tightening in her shoulders, a shift in the musculature of her face. Tension in the eyebrows where none existed before. I think I've plucked the right string.

She's expertly cutting a cucumber, breaking it down into neat, diced squares.

"What did you find?" Sam says, no trace of a reaction in her voice.

"A lost puppy on the street," Erica says. "I couldn't help but scoop him up."

She puts her arms around my shoulders like I'm her new toy.

"You decided to come," Sam says to me.

"Not like I had a choice," I say, motioning toward Erica.

"Be careful," Sam says. "She's known for overfeeding her pets."

"I'm not concerned," I say.

"You should be. She's got a cat the size of a Macy's balloon," Sam says.

"Don't hate on my feline," Erica says. "He's a little pudgy is all."

Sam puffs out her cheeks, and Erica doubles over laughing.

Sam looks from Erica back to me, the tiniest hint of anger in her eyes. She goes back to chopping.

"What are you making?" Erica asks her.

"Israeli salad," she says.

"My favorite!" Erica says, snatching a cube of tomato out of the bowl. "It's like *pico de gallo* with a different accent. I just need something to wash it down."

"Soda is on the kitchen table," Sam says. "And the stash is—"

"In the stash drawer," Erica says. "Got it."

She goes to a pantry the size of a walk-in closet, opens the third drawer down, and removes a bottle of extra-virgin olive oil. She pours two fingers into a glass, then tops it off with lemonade.

"You're going to drink oil?" I say. "That's a new one."

"It's tequila," Erica says. "Sam's little trick. Pretty good, huh? It's like the CIA of booze."

"I'm afraid to ask what's in the vinegar bottle," I say.

Sam turns to me, the chef's knife in her hand.

"I could tell you," she says. "But then I'd have to kill you."

I look at the knife. The blade is wet, shiny, and dangerous. I calculate the striking distance from Sam to me. Six tile-lengths on the kitchen floor.

I'm within five.

I subtly take a step back.

Most people would not notice my adjustment, but Sam tracks me with her eyes.

"Are you scared of knives?" she says.

"Only if they're pointed at me," I say.

She puts the knife down.

"Maybe I should have asked if you're scared of me," she says.

I smile.

"I'm more scared of your father. What happens if he finds out we're drinking in his house?"

"What he doesn't know won't hurt him," Sam says.

"So he's here?" I say.

"Somewhere," she says. "He runs and hides during these things."

But where is he hiding?

"Anyway, don't worry about the booze," Sam says. "It's not like the cops are going to come. They're already here."

"Buzzkill," Erica says. She takes a big gulp of spiked lemonade. *"Delicioso!"*

A group of girls passes by, and Erica lets out a whoop.

"I have to say hello to these bitches," she says with a grin. "Don't go far, little puppy, okay?"

She doesn't wait for an answer, just pinches my ear, then drifts off toward the music with drink in hand.

"You made a new friend," Sam says.

"I guess so."

"That was quick."

She stares me down.

I want her to be a little jealous, but I don't want to lose her. I need to be cautious with her now.

I say, "Is it okay that I came with her? I didn't want to be the new guy here all alone."

Sam waves me off.

"It's fine. It's a party. It's not like we had a date or anything."

"Not yet at least."

She grins and hands me a glass of the spiked lemonade.

"Any chance of your father walking in on me drinking this? I'd hate to make a bad first impression."

"You want to meet him, don't you?"

"Maybe."

"Don't lie to me. I hate that."

"I want to meet him. Why wouldn't I?"

She looks away from me, sips from her own lemonade.

"But I'd rather meet you," I say.

She looks back.

"Nice save."

"It's not a save. It's the truth."

"Maybe I'll introduce you sometime, Benjamin. If you and I—"

"If we what?"

"Get closer."

Closer. The word sounds good when she says it.

But I don't get closer to people. Not in the way she means.

I get closer to my target.

"You'd better find your date," Sam says.

"You mean before she goes on a rampage?"

"Some women get angry when they don't get their way."

"How about you?"

"I'm half Israeli," she says. "I get more than angry."

"I'll be sure to stay on your good side," I say.

And I go back to the party.

But it's not my date I'm looking for.

THE MAYOR IS HERE.

That's what Sam said. He's sequestered somewhere in the apartment.

I do a slow lap around the space.

I look around like I'm scouting for friends, but in fact I'm searching for the mayor and memorizing the terrain at the same time.

Two things I need to know:

How to get in, and how to get out again.

I note entrances and exits, doors, corners, blind spots. The weather is nice, so the windows are open. I step into an empty room and pop my head outside.

We're on the twelfth floor. It's a long way down.

There's a concrete molding that runs along the outside edge of the windows. Nothing you'd want to stand on for long.

I pull my head back inside, and Darius, the Shaggy Giant, is behind me, looking at me like he's got bad things on his mind.

"You thinking about giving me a push?" I say.

"I was hoping you were suicidal and I wouldn't have to."

"I am feeling a little sad today."

"Go with it," he says. "A little sad can become very sad. Especially when mixed with alcohol."

"You're a sweet guy. Sam was right."

The muscles in his shoulders clench.

"She was talking about me?" He looks intrigued for just a second, then he covers it. "No. She's not talking about me. Not to you. Nice try."

"You're right," I say. "She barely mentioned you."

Now his eyelid flutters.

High-strung guy. I don't want to deal with him now, not when I'm here for the mayor. I've already pushed him enough to get the upper hand. Now it's time to smooth things over a little. If something goes down tonight, I don't want him to be the one who says to the police, "Did you interrogate the new guy yet?"

"You need a drink?" I say, offering him my lemonade.

"Did you spit in it?"

"That's elementary school stuff. We're in the big leagues now. I pissed in it."

His eyes widen.

"I'm kidding. It's perfectly fine. I just don't drink."

I hold out the cup. Peace offering.

He hesitates.

"You in the program?" he says.

The Program.

Mother's image flashes in my head.

But he's not talking about my program. He's talking about AA. Alcoholics Anonymous.

"In and out," I lie. "But I gave up the drinking. Couldn't handle it."

"Sucks for you, huh?"

He sips from the lemonade.

"Obviously I don't have a problem," he says. "But I'm careful about it. You know how it is."

"Sure, sure," I say.

"Unlike you," he says. "You're not being careful."

"What are we talking about?"

"Sneaking into the party."

"I didn't sneak in. Your girl invited me," I say.

"She's not my girl. She's her own girl—er—woman."

"Your woman invited me. So whatever you told her after class didn't work."

"Hey, dude, it's not personal. She sent me to check you out. I told her what I thought."

"She sent you?"

"I don't know how you Choaties did it, but we have a code here. We take care of our own. Especially Sam. She's like royalty."

This guy's got it bad. It's pretty obvious.

He takes another sip. More than a sip. Half the glass is gone.

"How did you get in with her so quickly?" he says.

"I'm not in."

"You're in the house. It's hard to get in this house."

"It took you a while to get here, huh?"

"That's not what I meant."

He stares at me. Or tries to stare. His eyes are fuzzing out.

This is the real reason why I don't drink. Situational awareness is progressively diminished with substances in your system.

Plus, it just makes you stupid.

He takes another long gulp. Liquid courage.

"You," he says.

He points at me again. He loves to point. I'm starting to think this guy is a one-trick pony.

"I'm watching you," he says.

"You don't need to watch me," I say. "We're on the same side."

"We are?"

He sways a little on his feet.

"I'm not going to hurt Sam," I say. "I promise you."

He nods, and his guard goes down. "She's been through a lot, you know? I try to protect her, but it isn't easy."

I pat his shoulder. It's rock-hard from working out.

"I hear you," I say, heading toward the door.

"You want your drink back?" he says.

"It's all yours," I say.

He holds it up in a silent toast.

"See you around," he says.

Maybe not, I think.

ERICA GRABS ME BY THE ARM AND PULLS ME DOWN THE HALL.

No hello. No comment at all.

She sees me when I step out of the room, and she lunges. Actually, her dress is a little short for lunging, so it resists. Especially around the hips.

"I have to find someone," I say, trying to pull away from her.

"Someone more important than me?" she says.

"Of course not," I say. "I just need to—"

"Two seconds," she says. "I want to show you something."

She yanks me into the bathroom and slams the door behind us.

"What do you want to show me in here?"

"I brought you a present," she says.

She slurs her words. How much lemonade could she have had in fifteen minutes?

I look at her eyes.

Too much, I think.

"Where's my present?" I say.

She touches a finger to her lips.

"I don't get it."

"My mouth," she says. "That's your present."

"Your mouth?"

"I can do a lot of things with my mouth."

"You're on the debate team?"

"Hardy har-har," she says.

She leans in quickly, pushing me back against the sink and kissing me roughly. I taste a mix of tequila and sugar on her lips. It's like kissing a margarita.

A delicious one.

"See what I mean?" she says. "I can kiss with it—"

She leans in and bites my shoulder. "I can bite with it—"

She starts to kneel down in front of me.

"Whoa," I say. "Hold up."

It's not like I've never fooled around on a mission. If it would help me integrate into a social group or it gets me closer to my mark, I'd consider it. But I'm questioning how useful it would be in this situation.

Besides, there's something about Erica, something beneath the tough exterior, that has me wanting to tread carefully with her.

"You're being a prude, Ben. Benji."

"I'm not a prude. I think you're drunk."

"I'm buzzed. What's the big deal?"

I'm guessing buzzed is how she makes all her dating decisions. And I'm betting they don't turn out well, either.

"I don't want you to do anything you'll regret," I say.

"Like what, go down on you? Why would I regret that?"

Certain regions of my body would love to be swayed by that reasoning, but I resist.

I take her by the shoulders and bring her back to standing.

"Is it because of Sam?" she says.

She looks at my face.

"It is, isn't it? You lied to me before," she says.

"It's got nothing to do with Sam."

"Let me tell you something. You think she's Little Miss Superstar—everybody does—but you don't know her like I do. She's got a checkered past, Ben."

"Doesn't everybody?"

"Not me. I've got a checkered present. It's a lot better. All my shit's on the surface."

This isn't working. I have to try a different tack.

"The truth is that I can't get involved with anyone right now," I say.

"Neither can I," she says. "You asked if Sam has a boyfriend, but you didn't ask if I did. For your information, his name's Geoffrey. He's older. He goes to Princeton, and he would beat the crap out of you if he were here. What do you think about that?"

What's the right thing to say here?

"It scares me," I say.

"But it excites you, too, doesn't it?" She reaches for my belt.

I guess that was the wrong thing to say.

I take her hands in mine and hold on to them.

"Seriously. I don't want to mess with another guy's action."

"Are you noble or something?"

"It's not that."

"If that's what it is, then you're the only one in school," she says. "Nobody else cares."

"I care."

She stops grabbing at me, takes a large step back.

"Why?"

"I don't like taking advantage of people."

The line surprises me. Not because it's a line, but because when I say it, it feels like the truth.

Erica studies my face.

"You do care in some weird way," she says.

What is she seeing right now?

The whole thing is disturbing to me. The thoughts I'm having, the fact that I'm saying them out loud.

It's bad timing. *And it all started with Sam.*

"Love does terrible things to you," Erica says.

She pulls her skirt up to her waist. I see a flash of pink flowers on her underwear.

"What are you doing?"

"I need to pee," she says.

"I'll give you a little privacy."

"You don't have to," she says.

I slip out the door.

"You can run but you can't hide," she calls after me.

You'd be surprised, I think.

MUSIC ECHOES THROUGH THE HALL.

I move away from it, away from Erica and Darius, from Sam in the kitchen, from the party.

And toward the mayor.

I project my energy through the space the way I've been taught. Then I follow my intuition deeper into the apartment.

The music grows distant as I walk farther down the hallway, passing from public space into private. I scan the ceiling, looking for telltale signs of cameras—ceiling trim that has been added to cover wires or variations in the paint where holes have been patched after an install. I don't see any, but they could be there.

To protect myself, I move like a kid lost. If someone stops me, I can say it's my first time in the apartment. It wouldn't be unusual that I'd take a wrong turn, or even try a little sightseeing. It's the mayor's place, after all.

But I don't intend to be stopped.

I turn a corner and notice light spilling from a doorway down the hall.

I move toward it.

The door is open a crack, so I peek inside.

It's a well-decorated home office, the desk covered with papers and huge stacks of computer printouts. The desk light is on, filling the room with a golden glow. There's an overstuffed armchair facing the window, the back of a man's head, a shock of gray-brown hair.

"Hello?" I say.

The man doesn't turn.

I make my voice unassuming.

"Sorry to bother you," I say. "I think I'm lost."

"You found the only place in the apartment where the party *isn't*," the man says.

That's my opening.

"To be honest, that's the kind of place I was looking for."

"Why is that?"

"I don't really know anybody at the party."

"Then you are welcome here," the man says.

The voice. The haircut.

I make myself sound surprised.

"Oh my gosh. You're the mayor."

"So they tell me."

I reach into my breast pocket, feel for the ballpoint pen I brought with me.

"This is really embarrassing," I say. "I must have taken a wrong turn."

Laughter from the far end of the hall where I came from. Two kids from school go by, talking loudly and slapping each other too hard on the back.

"Join me if you like," the mayor says.

A slight accent. Manhattan by way of Jersey.

"Maybe for a minute," I say. I reach for the door. "Open or closed?"

"Close it. Give my head a rest."

"Perfect," I say.

I close the door. You can hear the faint rumbling of a bass line vibrating through the floor as I step into the room.

"Much better," the mayor says.

I calculate the odds. Chance of our being interrupted. Chance of my leaving the party early without attracting notice. Chance of the mayor passing away unexpectedly at a party where I happen to be.

Me, a new student. A stranger who has been here for less than a day.

It could be a mistake to act now. There must be no connection between me and the mayor's death, and my disappearance afterward can raise no red flags.

I have to constantly gauge this in my work. When am I integrated enough into the social system to act without drawing attention? Sometimes I finish quickly and I'm gone before anyone knows I was there, sometimes I wait for an opening, and other times—

Other times fate makes the decision for me.

The mayor turns, and I see his face for the first time, one side lit by the desk lamp, the other in darkness.

It is a kind face. A famous face.

And the eyes. Something about them.

Sam has the same eyes.

No matter. We are in this room together. The door is closed.

I need only to complete my assignment and be back at the party before anyone discovers the body.

"How many apartments do you think we can see from here?" the mayor says.

He turns and gazes out the window.

I look out at a gorgeous, unobstructed view of the city over the roof of the Museum of Natural History. Windows above, windows below. Life framed and illuminated in neat squares.

"Thousands, maybe," I say. I'm standing behind him, a few feet from his left shoulder.

"On the order of twelve thousand," the mayor says.

"You've counted them?"

"I don't need to. I count the number of windows viewed through a one-inch square of windowpane, then multiply by the overall size of the pane, then divide by the average number of windows per apartment."

"This is why you run the city and I'm failing trig."

He laughs.

I remove the pen. I spin it in my fingers without looking at it, find the trigger mechanism under my thumb.

"Twelve thousand in this one small slice of the city," the mayor says. "Imagine you were looking for an apartment. With so many choices, how could you choose the right one for you?"

My father's image pops into my head. My father in his office at the university. He'd take me to work occasionally, and I'd sit across from him while he graded papers at his desk. He'd look up from time to time and ask me a question—about life, relationships, school—and we'd argue back and forth about it. Even when I was ten years old he was training me how to think.

The mayor turns and looks at me.

"Most people don't get to choose," I say. "I mean, how many of those places can an average person afford?"

"Good point," the mayor says.

He looks back out the window. I take a step closer.

The music changes. The bass slows.

Thump, thump.

"So you're saying we don't choose," the mayor says. "Our limitations choose for us."

"I think so. Yes."

I remember Sam in the debate this morning. She has the same kind of intellectual curiosity. Now I know where she gets it from.

The mayor says, "But if your limitations make the choices for you, how do you know what it is you want?"

"Maybe it doesn't matter what you want," I say.

I take another step closer to the back of the mayor's neck.

Striking distance.

"And yet we are defined by our desires," the mayor says. "If you don't know what you want, how can you know who you are?"

"I guess you make your best choice given your circumstances, and then you live with it."

I twist the pen cap to the right.

It is weaponized. One click death, two clicks temporary coma.

"Maybe you're right," he says.

I click the pen once, and the pen point glides out, small and deadly.

"There is always a moment before you choose, isn't there?" the mayor says. "A moment when you realize the choice you're about to make could affect a number of people."

"Your choices, maybe. Not mine."

"Why is that?"

"You're the mayor. I'm just a teenager."

"Yet we all make choices. And they have repercussions."

Choices.

My father made a choice. He chose loyalty to one thing over another. *Questionable loyalty*, as Mother put it, and his choice changed my life forever.

I make choices, too, and I change other people's lives forever.

Sam's life, for example. And the mayor's.

I freeze with the pen in my hand.

Why am I thinking about this now?

A single step and I will be at the mayor's neck. I will be finished. I will be moving again, away from this city, this place, from Sam.

A single step.

I do not take it.

The mayor sighs. He turns toward me.

"You're very kind to put up with me," he says. "As you see, I've got a lot on my mind, and a very big decision to make about my future. Sorry to bore you with it."

"It's not boring," I say. "Just a little beyond me."

"Somehow I doubt that," he says.

He looks at my hand.

"Why do you have a pen?" he says.

At that moment the office door opens and Sam steps in.

"What are you doing in here?" she says.

I stare at her for a second, surprised to have been caught with the mayor.

I hesitated, and now my opportunity is gone.

I twist the pen cap to the left. Safe mode.

Sam waits, her hands on her hips.

"What am I doing?" I say. "I was about to embarrass myself by asking your father for an autograph."

"This is a private part of the residence. You shouldn't be here," Sam says.

"I invited him in," the mayor says. "And we had an excellent discussion, didn't we?"

"We did," I say.

The mayor throws me a wink.

"Okay. Sorry," Sam says.

The mayor walks toward Sam, his lanky body a little stiff. Sam gives him a big hug.

"My daughter is very protective," the mayor says. "Do you know her, son?"

I am not your son.

"My name is Benjamin," I say. "And I'm just getting to know her. There are a lot of layers."

The mayor laughs. He has a warm, easy laugh.

"Indeed, Benjamin," he says. "She's just like her mother that way."

"Hey, guys, I'm in the room," Sam says. "I can hear what you're saying."

I glance at the desk. A picture of the three of them—Sam, the mayor, and her mother, the woman whose picture I saw in the Facebook profile. They're all posed in front of a monument somewhere in the Middle East.

Sam says, "Why don't we get out of your way, Dad. I know you've got work to do."

She starts to pull me from the room.

"Just a minute," the mayor says.

He comes toward me. He holds out his hand, palm up.

"Your pen," he says. "Give it to me."

I take out the pen, click open the point.

I place it in his hand.

Gently.

He leans across his desk, pulls out a card with the mayoral logo. He shakes the pen. Then he uses it to write something. He folds the card up and passes it back to me.

"Nice to meet you, Ben," the mayor says.

"You, too, sir," I say.

We shake. His palm is warm and dry.

"I hope it won't be the last time," he says.

"I'm sure it won't."

I take two steps toward the door, then I stop.

"Sorry to bother you, sir, but my pen—"

He looks back toward his desk. The pen is sitting there.

"Of course," he says.

He hands it back to me.

THE PRO IS STANDING OUTSIDE THE OFFICE DOOR.

Waiting.

How long has he been here?

What if I had finished my assignment and walked out to find him here?

But that doesn't matter now.

The Pro looks at Sam, then at me.

"You're not allowed in this part of the residence," he says to me.

"This is my friend Benjamin," Sam says.

He talks to Sam, but he doesn't take his eyes off me.

"What were you doing in your father's office?" he says.

"Talking to my father. Privately." She emphasizes the last word.

He looks at Sam, nods, then cracks the door and peeks in, checking to make sure the mayor is in there.

"Satisfied?" she says.

"Just doing my job, ma'am."

He closes the door and goes back to his gargoyle impression.

Sam pulls me in the opposite direction.

"Asshole," she says. "Sorry about that."

"I don't think he likes me," I say.

"He doesn't like anyone," she says, "but he *really* doesn't like you."

"Strange, because I'm very likable."

"My father seems to think so."

"And you?"

"I haven't made up my mind yet."

"Take your time," I say. "I'm not going anywhere."

I can't go anywhere. I've wasted my first chance and I have to scramble to find another. I told Father I was going to finish quickly and make things simple. Instead I've screwed up and now things are getting more complicated.

I sense myself drifting into thoughts that are not helpful to me. Regret. Recrimination. I've learned not to dwell on such thoughts.

Things happen.

Adjust. Stay on task.

"Was my dad talking your ear off in there?" Sam says as we walk down the hall together.

"Both ears."

"He has a big decision to make, and it's got him a little crazy."

"Is he going to change garbage day to Thursday?"

"Funny," she says, "but it's more like, 'What am I going to do with the rest of my life?'"

"I didn't know mayors thought about things like that."

"Mayors in their final terms do," Sam says. "That's the beauty of term limits. They are fear-inducing."

"I thought he'd go back to running his company."

The mayor's company, GRAM. Global Risk Assessment Modeling. Sophisticated data-mining algorithms applied to global security. It turned the professor into a businessman and the businessman into a billionaire. That billionaire became the city's mayor at a time when the world felt the most unsafe.

At least that's how the story is told. That was nearly eight years ago. I was in third grade at the time.

"Who knows what he'll do," Sam says. "My father has a way of making simple things very complicated. My mother used to call him on that, but now—" Her smile fades. "Now we're sort of on our own."

Her mother. I'm remembering the article I read about her mother's car accident in Israel.

Sam stares at the ground, traces the pattern on the marble with one toe.

"You okay?" I say.

"Memories," she says. "I hate them sometimes."

"Me, too."

"Really? What do you have memories of?"

Many things, all of them dangerous to me.

Before I can answer, a girl with bright red hair interrupts us coming down the hall.

"Great party!" she says.

"Thanks for coming," Sam says to her.

Red gives me a double take, not recognizing the new guy with Sam. She lingers, waiting for an introduction.

She doesn't get one.

"I'll leave you guys alone," she says, and keeps going down the hall.

"Any other questions about my dad?" Sam says.

"A lot more," I say.

Her face darkens.

"I want to know more about him because I want to know more about you."

"I see," she says, studying my face.

"You're always trying to figure out if I'm telling the truth," I say.

"Professional hazard."

"What profession is that?"

"Daughter of a famous person," she says.

But I wonder if it isn't something else. *Girl who got hurt by her ex.* Or maybe *Girl who lost her mother and doesn't trust the world.*

Whatever it is, it's complicated.

We cross the threshold of the front door on the way back to the party, and I stop and grab the door handle.

I'm not going to get another opportunity with the mayor tonight. My best play is to get out now.

"Where are you going?" Sam says.

"I'm leaving."

"April Fool's?"

"For real."

"You're blowing off my party?"

"Not blowing it off. I was here; now I'm leaving."

This is not a girl who is used to boys walking away from her. I see her wrestling with the idea. She wants to ask another question, but she stops herself.

"Okay, then," she says. "But I think Erica will be disappointed."

"I have a habit of disappointing women," I say.

She twists a strand of hair between her fingers.

"And I have a habit of disappointing men. Something else we have in common."

I go out the door, past the suit posted there.

I listen as I walk down the hall, measuring off the seconds before she closes the door. With a friend, you might close it right behind them. With someone you're interested in, you might wait a few seconds before closing. And with someone you're falling for—

"Hey, Benjamin," she calls.

I look back, and she's standing halfway out the door, one hand on the knob, the door still open.

With someone you're falling for, you don't go inside. You wait and watch them go. Just like she's doing now.

"You haven't disappointed me," she says.

The elevator door opens. The operator waits.

"I haven't disappointed you yet," I say.

But I will when I kill your father.

She smiles and waves good-bye.

I step inside the elevator and let the doors close behind me.

I HAVE TO SIGN OUT IN THE LOBBY.

I make a checkmark next to my name, and the cops tell me to have a good night.

A nondescript kid taking off from the party.

That's how I want it.

I scan the street. My body remains casual, but I am very aware of my surroundings. I move, then pause, checking for reactions in the world around me.

There is nothing.

As I wait for the light to change at the corner, I pull the mayor's card from my pocket. The seal of the City of New York is embossed at the top.

In a neat scrawl the mayor has written:

> To my new friend—
> Great to meet you,
> Jonathan Goldberg

False familiarity. A politician's trick, but a good one.

A normal person would be swayed by a card like this. At the very least, the mayor would have just earned a vote for life.

I'm too young to vote, so the charm offensive is wasted on me.

Almost wasted.

Something about the mayor's energy stays with me. His image lingers after I've closed my eyes.

I think about him, then I think about Sam. The way she hugged her father.

I think about the fact that she lost her mother. Soon she will lose her father, too.

So be it. I did not make the choice.

A horn honks, snapping me back into the moment. I look up in time to see a black sedan cut off a cab. On the cab's roof, the ad reads:

Home is where the ♥ is.

The heart accelerates and disappears down the avenue.

I walk in the opposite direction.

I lost my home.

The thought appears like a strange, foreign thing.

I push it away.

I walk faster, feel the wind blow through my hair. I breathe in the motion of the city, the motion of the world, all of it spinning and moving and never stopping.

I am moving, too. I am moving and never stopping, one assignment after the next.

The thought gives me peace.

Briefly.

Because a half block down, I sense something. I glance in a store window, scanning the street behind me.

A black sedan. It's moving slowly in my direction, tailing me from two blocks back.

Is it the same sedan that cut off the cab a moment ago? I can't tell.

But I will find out.

I walk up to 86th Street and take a left toward Broadway. A busy street, traffic flowing. There's no way to accomplish a slow tail in this situation.

The sedan doesn't try. It accelerates into traffic and shoots past me. The windows are blacked out, so I can't see the driver. It turns up Broadway and disappears.

Maybe it wasn't after me in the first place.

I wait at the light, then I cross Broadway and keep going, walking along 86th Street.

I project my attention in all directions.

I don't sense anything.

Not for a full minute. That's when the sedan appears again, this time in front of me, speeding in my direction.

I put the pieces together. I was followed after meeting Sam, and now after leaving the mayor's. It's not a coincidence.

On my walk earlier, I noticed a construction Dumpster in front of a town house that's being renovated. I'm ten feet away from it.

I don't wait for the sedan to make its move. I cut hard right and leap across the sidewalk and behind the Dumpster. I race up to the brownstone and use my shoulder to push against the wood planking on the front door.

The wood groans and the padlock gives way with a loud snap.

I ENTER A DARK, DEMOLISHED PARLOR ROOM.

Exposed walls, torn flooring, wires dangling from the ceiling. A beautiful home that's been gutted for renovation.

I drag over a dirty wheelbarrow, flip it sideways to prop the door from the inside.

Footsteps on the sidewalk in front of the brownstone. Two players, maybe more.

They walk past, then double back. I have to move quickly.

There's a staircase to my left with the banister missing.

Up or down?

There's a chance I could get trapped on higher floors, but it's a small risk compared to the benefits. Elevation and surprise. Two key elements for repelling an attack.

I run for the stairs.

I make it to the second-floor landing before I hear the sound of the front door being forced. There are four levels in the residence, which means I'll likely find a living room and dining room on the second floor. I need space to fight, so it's here or the roof. I choose here.

I move quickly down the hallway until I arrive at a door with a thick plastic sheet taped across to prevent dust from entering the rest of the house. Maybe it's mold abatement. Maybe asbestos. You never can tell in these old buildings. The secrets behind the walls.

I pull the sheeting away from the door frame and enter a large living room. There's a streetlamp at window level outside, the light spilling across the center of the room, dividing the space into shadows and light.

A second later the plastic rustles at the doorway. I fling myself behind a column as the first man enters. I peek around the edge, monitoring his movements.

He is nervous. He peeks into the room, his head swiveling as he looks for me. I hold my breath, make my energy soft.

After a moment he exhales and starts to back out of the room.

He stops, looks down.

Dust on the floor, illuminated by the window. The imprints of the paper booties of the men who work in the room, their steps arranged in a well-worn trail.

Crossing them is something else. My shoe prints.

I didn't look down.

Stupid.

The man moves back into the room, following the footprints, looking for me. He snatches a pry bar off the floor and advances.

I wait for him to cross my path, moving to the other side of the column to get behind him. I let him get one step past and I strike, hooking him beneath his shoulder with one arm and clamping my hand over his mouth with the other.

The pry bar clangs loudly to the floor.

There's a reaction from the floor below us. A second set of footsteps rushes up the staircase.

I grip the man as he struggles in my arms. We spin around the room in an awkward dance. I catch glimpses of expensive wallpaper partially stripped during construction.

I imagine this space fully furnished, elegant and clean, a happy family moving in and out of the room as they go about their day.

But that was a different time.

Now there is violence. Now there is struggle.

The man in my arms bucks hard, trying to throw me off his back. I increase the pressure against his shoulder, feel the rotator cuff strained to its limit. I don't want to hurt him. Not if I don't have to. I need to know who he is, ask him questions.

A shadow crosses the plastic sheeting of the doorway and continues down the hall.

The man struggles harder in my arms, trying to get away, trying to shout out.

I clamp down on his mouth and pinch his nose at the same time, denying him air.

If the second man continues up the stairs, I'll temporarily knock this man out and go after number two.

But the second man does not move on. He comes back.

A figure appears behind the plastic. Not nervous like the man in my arms. The figure is powerful, sure of himself.

The Presence. He's back.

He assesses without entering the room, his face obscured through thick plastic.

Suddenly the man in my arms has a blade. It happens in an

instant. He shrugs his arm hard, and it appears from a hidden sheath on the inside of his forearm.

He stabs backward, aiming for my neck but settling for the shoulder if he can get it.

I turn quickly, and the blade flashes an inch from my face.

I was able to dodge the first time, but the second time I may not be so lucky.

I do not kill for sport, only when necessary.

I quickly assess my options.

It is necessary.

I shift my hand rapidly from his mouth to his forehead, readying a killing blow.

In the split second that his mouth is uncovered, he shouts out. I immediately torque his head viciously to the side until his spine snaps, and he goes limp in my arms.

A single phrase. That's all he has time to shout. It's a foreign phrase, but one I recognize from my training.

A warning.

In Arabic.

I let his body fall and I rush toward the Presence, whipping the plastic sheeting out of my way.

But he's gone.

I hear footsteps at the bottom of the stairs, followed by the slap of wood as the Presence bursts through the front door.

He's got too much of a head start. By the time I make it outside, I'll have no chance at all.

I head back toward the room, checking the hallway floor as I go.

I see my footprints and those of the man inside the room.

I also see a third set, from the Presence.

Boot treads in the dust. Brand-new boots. Not worn in.

I go back inside to examine the man I just killed.

I drag his body toward the shaft of light coming through the window. I examine him head to toe. New clothes. A starchy jersey, khakis, stiff new work boots.

New everything.

Professionals do not buy new clothes for a job. It's too hard to age them correctly. New shoes will slip if they're not scuffed. New sneaker treads will stick. All of it will pop on visual inspection.

These guys move like they're military, but trained professionals do not buy new clothes. Not unless they have to because they're in a rush.

Rushed.

Like me. Like my assignment.

I think about the man speaking Arabic.

There are no coincidences on assignment. That's what Mother taught me.

Sam's mother was Israeli. She died in the Middle East.

The men are speaking Arabic.

It's a tenuous connection, but it's something that needs exploration.

The question now is, how am I going to explore it?

I DREAM OF HOUSES.

The one where I grew up, the one where I trained. And a third one. The mayor's residence.

One becomes the other in the dream. I am lost inside of these spaces, trying to find my way. I use my training, marking walls, memorizing turns, doing what I know to do.

But it all fails. The harder I struggle to get my bearings, the more lost I become.

I wake from the dream, my breath coming in gasps.

I sit up in bed, trying to understand what's happening. I don't dream on assignment, not like this.

I dream plans. I dream strategy. I dream about finishing.

But this dream, what was it about?

Failing.

That's not possible.

I run to the bathroom and splash water on my face. I look at my reflection in the bathroom mirror.

What's happening to me?

A double vibration from my phone. It's the signal for a secure call request from Father.

I glance at the clock.

6:45 AM. Day 2.

I take the call.

"How was the party last night?" Father says. No greeting.

"It was very interesting," I say.

I think of the body in the town house. I did not send a weather advisory to alert a cleanup crew. I'd have to explain myself to The Program, allow that my cover had been blown, and with it, possibly my entire assignment.

I've never blown an assignment, and I've never been discovered.

It will not happen this time. I will figure this out, and I will finish.

I'm quite sure of it.

So I did not signal a weather alert, and I will not discuss it with Father now.

My guess is that the body is no longer there. It feels like the Presence is military, and now I know he's not working alone. He would not leave a body around if it threatened him in any way.

"Did you get to meet the mayor?" Father says.

Odds he knows I met the mayor, that there's someone in the house reporting to him?

Low.

Necessity of testing this hypothesis by lying to him?

Also low. Stick to facts.

"I met him," I say.

And I hesitated.

I do not say that.

"Am I going to read about it in the *Times*?" Father says.

"No."

A pause.

"That's my other line," he says. "I'll call you right back."

The connection cuts off.

I'm in trouble.

I met the mayor, and the mayor isn't dead. Father wants to know why.

A text message comes in on my phone.

Great talking to you.
—Dad

This is no normal text message. I press it, and my touch brings up the front-facing camera. I'm staring into the phone at a live video feed of myself.

The video stream is open to Father. He can see me, but I can't see him.

"Was there a problem last night?" Father says.

"No problem," I say. "My meeting the mayor does not make the *Times*, Dad. Students often meet the mayor."

"Not students like you. Not special students."

"Special students, normal students, all kinds of students. There were a lot of people at the residence last night. It was hard to get any time alone with the mayor."

"I see."

Silence on the line.

I've got a pretty good idea why. Father is running my image

through microexpression software, monitoring my eye movement, subtle changes in my facial musculature, the number of times I blink per minute.

In other words, a lie detector.

Which is bad news for me, because I'm lying.

I've never lied to Father before. Why now?

He said this is a test. My greatest test yet.

And what do I want the results to be?

Am I a soldier or a boy who hesitates? Who can't handle a presence following him? Who has memories when he should be focused on his task?

No.

I am a soldier.

And a soldier finishes the mission.

So I don't tell Father the details of last night. I concentrate on making my face calm on the screen. I slow my breathing. I imagine the muscles in my face—relaxed and untroubled, professional in every way.

"My concern is that meeting the mayor is a once-in-a-lifetime event," Father says.

"It was very special," I say. "But that doesn't mean it won't happen again. Remember, I'm going to school with his daughter now."

"You're telling me you may meet him again," Father says. "If you're lucky."

"We make our own luck," I say. "Isn't that what you taught me?"

"It is," he says.

I shift on the edge of the bed. I feel the indentation caused by someone else's body. On every assignment there is a mattress perfectly broken in. How do they do it? I imagine a giant device slamming into the bed over and over again, bending fabric and padding to its will.

Father says, "If you need anything, you'll let me know?"

"Of course."

"Do you need anything?"

I sense him looking at me on the other side of the phone. Looking at my image as it is analyzed by a computer.

"I have everything I need," I say.

"That's my boy," he says, and the line disconnects.

I'M AT A COMPUTER IN THE SCHOOL LIBRARY.

I'm surfing the Web, sitting in a carrel in a long row of computers. Most students at this school carry laptops, netbooks, or iPads. But they also provide computers in the library for those who might need one.

I do not need one, of course. I have my phone, and my phone is secure, at least to the world at large. But it might not be secure from The Program.

And I do not want The Program to know what I am doing.

Investigating.

In a strict sense, I do not need additional information to complete my assignment. My job is not to investigate or understand the big picture. I have a name, I have a target, and I have my training. That should be enough.

In a normal assignment it is. But things are happening that are not normal.

The Presence. Who is he and where did he come from? How could he know that I am here?

The man last night shouted to him in Arabic.

Sam's mother was Israeli, and she died in her home country.

The Middle East. That is the connection.

It's a long shot. But it's something.

As I surf, I focus especially on stories about the mayor losing his wife. Her car accident in Israel. I read article after article about the tragedy. I look at photos of the aftermath.

One in particular gets my attention.

It's a picture of Sam at the funeral. Her father is next to her, side by side with the Israeli prime minister. Behind them is a group of soldiers standing at attention. They stare straight ahead.

All except one.

He looks at Sam.

It could be the angle of the shot. A coincidence of timing. A sneeze. Someone passing by in the street he recognizes.

Or it could be something else, something to do with Sam.

The picture is grainy, the soldier's features unclear. Yet there is something familiar about this man.

"How did you like the party?" Howard says.

He comes over and sits next to me. I casually click the browser closed before he can see it.

"The party was okay," I say. "Were you there?"

"I was invited, but I didn't go."

"Why not?"

"I don't go to parties."

"Is there a reason?"

"People are there."

"What's wrong with people?"

"I don't get along with them," Howard says. "Not the ones in this school."

"Only Sam," I say.

"Only Sam."

He looks toward the ground. He's always looking at the ground. I've seen this before. In animals who have been hurt.

I say, "Wouldn't it be worth suffering through a party just to be at the mayor's place?"

He shrugs.

"I was there a few years ago," he says. He looks up at me. "Did you see Sam's room?"

"Why would I see her room?"

"I don't know. On the tour or whatever."

A loud yawn from a student across the room.

I scan the space. Is anyone listening to us? Giving us too much attention?

No.

"Why are you asking so much about the party, Howard?"

"I've never seen Sam like a guy so fast."

"What does it matter if she likes me?"

"I'm worried that you're up to something," he says.

"What could I be up to?"

"A conquest."

"Not my style."

Not strictly true. I don't have a style. I do what's necessary.

"Then maybe it's something else," Howard says. "Something to do with the mayor?"

I don't like where this conversation is headed. I consider the possibility of Howard having an accident in the men's room. How much attention would it draw?

Not much.

There would be a disruption, almost certainly a police investigation.

I decide an accident outside of school might be better. Better still is to remove the need for one.

"Okay, you caught me," I say.

"It's the mayor?" he says, leaning in.

"It's sex."

"Oh. Typical." He looks disappointed.

"Everyone wants to have sex with the mayor's daughter, right?"

"I don't," Howard says.

"No?"

"I don't think it's right to be friends with someone just because her father is famous. Unlike certain people in this school."

"You've never thought about being with Sam?"

He smiles a shy smile.

"I'm taken," he says.

"You have a girlfriend?"

He looks around to make sure we're not being overheard, then he motions for me to come closer. He flips open a netbook, and his fingers fly across the keys. The school might be wired for Internet, but Howard is wired for speed on the Internet.

In three seconds flat his screen is turned toward me.

An anime character stares out at me. She has enormous eyes. When she blinks, tiny rainbow-colored stars float from her lashes.

"This is Goji," he says. "She's my girlfriend."

"Goji like the berry?"

"It's a nickname."

"Um—is she an anime character?" I say.

"That's just her avatar," he says like I'm a little dense. "For your information, she's Japanese. And she's real. Hey, do you want to see *my* avatar?"

He doesn't wait for an answer. His fingers fly across the keys again, stopping when a Howard avatar pops up on-screen.

At least I think it's Howard. The hair is familiar, but everything else is transformed. Howard after five years in a gym and extreme makeover surgery.

His character waves at hers, the hand causing ripples of blue-green energy to flow outward. Suddenly the two characters run toward each other on the screen, meeting in an embrace that sends them both flying through the air on a river of hearts.

"She calls me Fro-Fro. Because of my hair. It's like an afro."

Goji and Fro-Fro. Cute. If you're into things like that.

"What does Goji look like in real life?" I say.

He looks down again. "I've never seen her. She lives in Osaka."

"Maybe you'll go someday," I say.

"Yeah, maybe," he says, like he doesn't believe it. "That would be nice."

I thought Howard might be a rival for Sam, at least in his head. But now I see I was wrong. He's a potential confidant.

"Does Sam have anyone?" I say.

"Not right now."

"But in the past."

His fingers fly over the keys again. He pushes the screen toward me. It's a *Daily News* article from a couple of years ago. A single column inch buried deep in the paper.

Body Found in Harlem River

The body of a teenage boy who apparently committed suicide was found in the Harlem River, cops said.

"What does this have to do with Sam?"

"The guy in the river? He was a Bronx Science guy. He liked Sam."

"And he committed suicide?"

"That's what the paper said. But I don't think so."

"I'm not understanding you, Howard."

He lowers his voice.

"The guy went out with Sam a couple times, and then he ended up in the river."

"She killed him?" I say with a smile.

He shakes his head. He's not smiling.

"Who?" I say.

He glances around the room.

"She had a boyfriend at the time," he says.

"The ex you told me about who messed with her head?"

"That's right," he says. "It was a long-distance thing. He was Israeli. I don't know much more than that."

"I thought you and Sam were close."

"We talk about a lot of stuff, but she's very careful on that subject."

"So you think this Israeli guy killed him?"

"I can't prove anything. But he might have. It was that kind of relationship."

"What kind?"

"Intense."

"This guy," I say, "he's out of the picture now?"

"Sam says he is, but I'm not so sure," Howard says.

"Why not?"

"They broke up, but she keeps going back."

"Thanks for the info, Howard."

"Sure," he says. "It's sort of nice to have someone to talk to."

He looks at the floor again, the loneliness practically radiating off him.

I think of myself, waiting in hotel rooms all over the country, keeping busy by watching TV or walking through strange cities, never knowing the people around me, communicating only on my phone with people whom I never see in person.

"You're an okay guy, Howard."

"Really?"

"Did you ever think of taking a self-defense class or something?"

"I can't fight in real life. Only on the computer."

"You're a gamer?"

He looks around the library, makes sure nobody can hear him.

"No, but I like to mess around a little."

"Like hacking?"

He shrugs.

"I can do some things. For example, I cracked Justin's e-mail and signed him up for a herpes newsletter."

I laugh.

"I might be a loser in real life, but I'm a ninja online."

"That's good to know," I say.

"YOU THINK YOU GOT AWAY," ERICA SAYS.

I turn around like I'm surprised she's behind me in the hallway at school.

"Did I scare you?" she says.

"A little," I say.

She smiles, delighted with herself. I don't tell her I heard her heels clomping on the floor from fifty feet away.

"You did not get away," she says. "Nobody gets away."

"Nobody?"

"Not from me. I'm a hunter. When I see something I want, I go after it."

"And you always get it?"

"Always."

She runs her fingers like a claw through her chemically straightened hair.

Braggadocio—absurd confidence in her own sexuality. I could

shut this girl down quickly, go to that soft place inside and press. Release a flood of emotional pain.

For most people, emotional is worse than physical. I do not understand why this is, but I know how to use it to my advantage.

I could shut her down, but that would not be useful. I need to get back to the mayor's, and I need to do it fast. Maybe Erica can help.

So instead of calling her out, I say, "Erica."

"Benjamin."

"Your hair looks nice today."

Her head cocks to the side, uncertain of my intentions. She studies my face, one hand propped on her hip, like a model.

"Flattery will get you everywhere," she says.

"Will it get me a chance to walk you to class?"

"It will."

She slips her arm into mine. Another of her favorite tricks. And just what I was hoping for.

"Did I embarrass myself last night?" she says.

"Not at all."

"That's nice of you to say."

"I did see your underwear."

"What did you think?"

"Floral."

She laughs and pulls me closer.

"How often does Sam have parties at her place?" I say.

"Once every couple years. Everyone wants to go because it's the mayor's place, but it's not that much fun. How can you party with cops everywhere?"

"I know what you mean."

When we get to the end of the hall, I lead her to the left.

"Why are we going this way?"

"Shortcut," I say.

"No, it's not."

"You got me. I took the long route so we'd have more time together."

"Benjamin, I'm not falling for it."

Maybe not. But she seems happy to be with me, which is the next best thing.

We walk down the hall, right past AP European.

Past Sam.

That's why I want Erica next to me. Sam is sitting where she always does in the front row. In full view of the door.

I slow our pace. Erica glances in and catches Sam's eye. She winks at Sam.

Perfect.

I've injected conflict between Sam and me where before there was closeness. I don't have time for this to develop slowly between us, and I've been taught that relationships are strongest when they have to overcome something in order to exist. Romeo and Juliet, for example. Take away the families at war, and what do you have? A weekend fling that ends with two kids bored of each other.

Conflict.

It makes all the difference in the world. And I'm betting on the fact that it will stir things in an interesting way with Sam.

When we get to her class, Erica says, "You wanted Sam to see us, didn't you?"

"Maybe," I say.

I don't deny it. She's too smart for that.

"I'm okay with it," she says. "You know why?"

"Why?"

"Because Sam is great, but I know I'm a better fit for you."

"Why is that?"

"You get me."

"Maybe I get her, too."

"Nobody gets her. I don't think she gets herself. And I love her, so I'm not saying it to be cruel."

"We'll see what happens," I say.

"Game on," she says, and she heads into class.

I double back to AP European. As I come around the corner, Sam is waiting in the hallway. She left class to confront me.

It's a good sign.

"Having fun?" she says.

"Lots," I say. I roll my eyes.

She's not amused.

"You're with Erica, then you're with me, then Erica again. Why do I feel like you're telling us both the same things?"

"I'm using her," I say.

"Why?"

"To get to you."

"And you think I'm going to be flattered by that? Big mistake. I hate games."

"Me, too."

"But you're playing them. Maybe that's all you know how to do."

Darius rushes down the hall, late for class. He sees us and slows down.

"Problem?" he says to Sam.

She looks at me.

"Yes, actually. Ben has a problem telling the truth."

"News flash: Ben is a dick," Darius says.

"I thought we bonded last night," I say, playing the hurt friend.

"Not if Sam has a problem with you we didn't. She comes first."

The second tone sounds.

"Shall we?" Darius says to Sam, gesturing toward the room.

He heads into class, Sam following behind.

"Wait, Sam—" I say.

She hesitates.

"I'm sorry."

"And?" she says.

"And I'm a dick. Darius is right."

"Don't waste your time with him," Darius says.

Darius lingers by the door. She puts a hand on his arm.

"I'm okay," she says.

He grunts and goes inside. She closes the door behind him.

"You're very mysterious, Ben."

"How so?" I say.

"What you want, who you are."

"I'm simple," I say. "What you see is what you get."

"I don't see. That's the problem. Usually I see everything. I'm very good at sniffing out the truth. But with you it's different. One minute I think I know what I'm seeing, the next I'm not so sure."

"What do you want to know?"

"What you like, what you don't. Your politics."

"My politics?"

"I'm a serious person. I want to be with a serious person."

Be with. What does she mean by that?

The last class tone sounds, but neither of us moves.

I think about how to play this.

Come at her with politics similar to hers. Bond.

Come at her with contrary politics. Opposites attract. *Get a reaction out of her.*

"You're calculating," she says.

"No, I'm not."

"I see you doing it. Why don't you just give me a straight answer."

A straight answer.

"Okay. Straight answer is that I'm not political."

"You don't care about the world."

"I care about myself in the world."

"Typical American attitude," Sam says.

"You're American, too."

"I live in America. But I don't feel American."

"What do you feel?"

"I feel . . . torn."

"Because of your mom?"

She winces.

"It has nothing to do with her," she says.

Obviously it does, but I don't need to push the issue now.

"I'm sorry I brought it up," I say.

She hits herself in the thigh. "Ugh, I'm so friggin' weird around you. I hate it."

I look at her, struggling to find the right thing to say.

A crack in the facade of Samara the Powerful. The first I've seen.

A sign that she's opening up to me.

"I don't think you're weird," I say.

Her face softens.

"Can I get a do-over on this conversation?" she says.

"Absolutely," I say. "As long as I can get a do-over on last night."

"What do you have in mind?"

"How about dinner at your place?"

"My place?" she says.

"It's a lot cleaner than mine."

She laughs.

"Actually, I'm having dinner with my father tonight. It's kind of a special night."

"Perfect. Your father loves me," I say.

"He kind of does," she says. "He asked about you this morning."

"What did he ask?"

"If there was anything going on between us."

"And what did you tell him?"

She smiles and looks toward the classroom door.

"We'd better get in there," she says.

"And dinner?" I say.

She doesn't answer, just opens the door, and motions me into class with a grand gesture.

I go in first. As I pass by, she whispers in my ear.

"Eight o'clock. Don't show up with Erica this time."

"Not a chance," I say.

THE POLICE BOX ON THE SIDEWALK IN FRONT OF THE MAYOR'S BUILDING IS MANNED.

A small, heated shack. One officer on duty.

I walk into the lobby and I recognize the downstairs staff from last night. The concierge announces me by phone.

As I ride up in the elevator, I'm thinking about last night.

How I hesitated with the mayor.

I decide it was a fluke, a "nonrecurring phenomenon." That's what Mother calls once-in-a-lifetime scenarios. I am trained for such things, trained to react to circumstances, adjust, and reapply myself.

That's what I'm going to do tonight. Reapply myself.

Day two of five. I don't intend to need the other three days.

One sticking point: the Presence.

My research turned up very little. I still don't know who the Presence and his team are working for, or what their intention is. If I complete my assignment tonight, will I have to contend with them?

I decide I'll cross that bridge when I get to it.

The elevator doors open, and I'm in the penthouse vestibule.

The Pro is there, waiting.

First obstacle.

"Hello again," I say.

No reaction.

Not quite true. No reaction for a second, and then he says, "Turn around and put your hands above your head."

"Why do I have to turn around?" I say.

"Because I'm going to search you," the Pro says.

I wonder what this is about. Is it standard operating procedure, or am I getting special attention because he's suspicious?

No matter. I have to react like a normal teen might. In this case, belligerently.

"You didn't search me last night," I say.

"Tonight's different."

"What about my civil rights?"

"This is not a discussion. Turn around, or walk back out the door."

"Whatever," I say.

I turn around and lift my arms.

I was anticipating this, or at least the possibility of it. I'm carrying a wallet with thirty bucks and a school ID. I'm wearing a watch. I've got a phone and a ballpoint pen.

That's it.

The Pro finds them all. Finds and dismisses.

"You're okay," he says.

But he still searched me. I'm going to need to leave quickly later, so I have to do some damage control.

"You here all the time?" I say.

"What do you care?"

I make my voice friendly. "I'm just wondering if you have a family."

He ignores me, knocks at the apartment door on my behalf.

We stand there waiting. He glances at me.

"I've got a family, but I don't see them much."

A moment of humanity. I can use this.

"No kids?" I say.

"I've got a son. He's in the military."

"Just like his father."

"Why are you asking so many questions? You want to be a soldier when you grow up?"

"I've thought about it."

"Don't do it. It's a tough life. You got a second choice?"

"Lawyer. They make bank."

He chuckles. That's a good sign. Let his last memory of me be of a funny kid he likes. It's going to make things easier.

Sam opens the door.

"Welcome back," she says.

She's wearing a simple print dress covered by a kitchen apron. No makeup, but it doesn't matter. She looks fabulous.

"Hey there," I say.

"Come in."

I glance back at the Pro. "Take care," I say, but he doesn't respond.

Sam shuts the door behind me. Her hair is freshly washed. I can smell the sweet scent of her shampoo as I pass by.

"I didn't know tonight was dressy," I say.

Her hand goes to the apron.

"Oh, this. I'm cooking."

"Do you know how?"

"I just learned this morning. I hope you have a strong stomach."

I smile, and she takes my coat. I slip my pen out before she does.

"Are you angling for another autograph?" she says.

"It's my lucky pen. I always carry it with me."

"Do you need luck tonight?"

"From what you say about your cooking? Maybe."

"Don't worry, you'll be okay. The truth is I like to cook. Family night, there's no staff around. Just Dad and me."

"And the Easter Island statue outside the door."

"He's new," she says. "They increased Dad's security a few weeks ago."

"Did something happen?"

"I can't really talk about it."

The mayor calls from down the hall, "Is that Benjamin?"

He comes puttering out, relaxed and slightly rumpled in a button-up sweater and khakis. You wouldn't know this was one of the richest men in the country.

"Welcome back," he says.

"I already said that, Dad."

"Great minds think alike."

"I'm going to check my sauce," Sam says. "Can you keep each other company for a few minutes?"

A few minutes. That might be enough time for me.

"I refuse to let you back in that kitchen," the mayor says. He heads toward the kitchen himself.

"Where do you think you're going?" Sam says.

"I want you to spend time with your friend."

"But my sauce," Sam says.

"I manage the city," he says. "I can probably keep your sauce from burning for ten minutes."

I say, "Don't you have deputy mayors for sauces?"

The mayor laughs. "I like your style," he says.

"Just make sure you keep stirring, Dad."

"Yes, ma'am."

He salutes and heads into the kitchen.

"Looks like we're stuck together," I say.

"As painful as that is," Sam says, and she grins at me. "Come on. I'll give you the grand tour."

"Didn't I get that last night?"

"If you're nice, I'll take you someplace you haven't been yet," she says.

"Where's that?"

"Don't ask so many questions," Sam says.

And then she leads me to her bedroom.

A HALF-DOZEN PICTURES OF HER MOTHER ARE FRAMED ON THE DRESSER.

There are more on the wall by her bed. Some show her mother alone; others show her posed with different family members.

"Your mom's everywhere," I say.

Is this why she brought me here? To show me this?

"It's good for me to have her pictures around," she says.

People keep photos of those they love. It comforts them. I know this, but I don't understand it. Not really.

"Why is it good?" I say.

"I feel like a part of her is here with me."

"A part of her. Is that enough?"

"Sometimes it is. And other times—"

She picks up one of the pictures. She's four or five years old in the photo, holding hands with her mother.

"You don't have pictures from your childhood?" Sam says.

"Not like you do."

One of the photos on the dresser catches my attention. Sam stands in a desert next to a young man in combat fatigues with an Uzi on his shoulder.

Not just any young man.

The same one I saw in the picture of Sam at her mother's funeral on the computer in the school library. The soldier who seemed to be staring at her.

"Who's this?" I say.

"Just some soldier. It was a photo op when we visited the Negev."

"A tourist thing, huh?"

"Exactly. What's a trip to Israel without a cool picture of a soldier with a gun?"

He's not just some soldier. He's in two separate photos with Sam taken at different times.

Which means she's lying to me.

The question is why.

I pick up the photo and tension immediately forms around her lips.

It's subtle, but I see it.

Sam is maybe thirteen or fourteen in the photo, the hint of a young girl still in her face. The soldier next to her is fierce-looking. He is around nineteen. Dark complexion, curly hair.

I recognize something about him.

Maybe it's his eyes. They're hard, like a soldier's.

"You're really into that picture," Sam says. She's nervous. I hear it in her voice.

"You look so young," I say.

"I was a babe in the woods. Actually, a babe in the desert."

"I noticed that. Looks like the soldier did, too."

Suddenly the nervousness is gone. She comes forward and takes the photo out of my hands.

"Are you jealous, Ben?"

"Of course I am. I wish I knew you back then."

"I wish you did, too," she says.

She puts the photo away and sits down on her bed. I sit next to her.

"All these pictures of your mother," I say. "Can I ask how she—"

"You didn't read about it?" she says.

"The paper and reality are two different things."

She hesitates, like there's something she wants to talk about, but she stops herself.

She says, "It was an accident. She was driving, and she got hit. It happened when we were in Israel."

"I'm sorry."

"Nothing to be sorry about. Life is like that."

"Filled with accidents?"

"Unfair," she says.

I think of the last time I was in my father's office at the university. He'd gone to a meeting and left me there for safekeeping. I sat on the sofa reading, content to be alone in his space, surrounded by my father's books and papers, believing that he would be back soon.

But he didn't come back.

The memory plays on a loop in my head.

The call that there had been an accident.

Running home to find Mike sitting at the kitchen table waiting for me.

A sensation passes through my body. A strange sensation. It causes a constriction in my chest and throat.

Sam is watching me.

"Have you ever lost someone?" she says.

"Maybe."

"It's hard for you to talk about, isn't it?"

I don't answer her.

She says, "If you ever want to talk to me about it—I've been there. That's all I'm saying."

"It was a long time ago," I say.

Sam looks at a picture of her mother holding up a baby with a pink barrette in its hair.

"It changes you, doesn't it?" she says.

"Yes."

"Kids!" Sam's father calls from the kitchen.

"He still thinks I'm a kid," Sam says. "How could I be a kid with everything that's happened?"

I breathe in and out. It is more difficult than it should be.

"Are you hungry?" Sam says.

"Very," I say.

It is a lie.

HER FATHER'S FOREARM IS EIGHTEEN INCHES AWAY ACROSS THE TABLE.

It's covered in light brown hair. Freckles dot the arm. The skin is pale from too much time spent indoors.

The arm reaches toward me to get the salt. It shifts from eighteen inches away to less than a foot.

"What are you thinking about, young man?" the mayor says.

I want to finish and get away from this place. That's what I'm thinking. I don't like what happens to me when I'm with Sam.

"I'm thinking how good this tastes," I say. "And how surprised I am, given the chef's inexperience."

Sam kicks me under the table.

The mayor's arm picks up the salt and retracts. It shakes the salt. It returns it to the center of the table.

"Despite what she tells you, Samara is a very good cook," the mayor says.

"Zabar's is a very good cook," Sam says.

183

"It might have started as Zabar's," the mayor says, "but you transformed it into Samara's."

"In that case I'll take partial credit," Sam says.

The mayor pulls a camera out of his pocket.

"I almost forgot," he says.

He points the camera, and I subtly lean back. I do not want pictures of me in this place, especially not tonight.

The mayor moves his plate a few inches closer, leans down, and takes a picture of dinner. The flash lights up the room.

"Dad," Sam says with a groan.

"Are you immortalizing our meal?" I say.

"It's for the Web," he says. "I'm posting about my real life—the things I do, the things I eat. Transparency comes to City Hall."

Sam says, "My dad's blogging. Can you believe it?"

The mayor passes me the camera.

I look at the picture of the dinner; the broccoli glows green in the light of the flash.

"When Sam suggested it, I thought it was a terrible idea," the mayor says. "But now that I'm doing it, it's kind of fun."

"It makes you seem like a human being," Sam says.

"Instead of what? The monster I really am?"

The Pro from the front door steps into the room. He doesn't signal his presence. He just appears.

The mayor notices him two seconds after I do.

"Do you need me?" the mayor says.

"I saw a flash," the Pro says.

"I'm taking pictures of my dinner," the mayor tells him.

I hand the mayor back his camera.

The Pro nods. "Sorry to bother you, Mr. Mayor."

"Carry on," the mayor says.

The Pro goes on with his rounds.

I've been here about forty-five minutes and he's doing rounds. I'm guessing he's on a once-per-hour schedule. Maybe less frequently given that there's nothing going on and triple-redundant security between the apartment and the street.

But to be cautious, I set a clock running for an hour in my head. Five minutes to finish his rounds, then an hour before I see him again.

"I hate all the security," the mayor says.

"You're not used to it by now?" I say.

"NYPD, yes. Our boys in blue when I go to an event. But people in my home? That's hard to get used to."

"Why do you need extra security?" I say.

Sam looks at her father but doesn't say anything.

"State secrets," the mayor says with a smile. Then he changes the subject. "Let's eat before it gets cold."

I let it go for now.

We dig in to dinner and Sam talks to her father about what's happening in school. Stories of grades and tests and the various personalities she deals with day to day. It occurs to me that this is a conversation thousands of kids probably have with their parents every day. Talking during a meal, sharing stories, questions asked and answered, other questions avoided.

It is the most natural thing in the world, but it is not something I do. My conversations are encoded communications, mission tasking, status updates. They are work-related only.

This is real. This is how these people live their lives.

You're not missing anything.

That's what I tell myself. Even a mayor talking to his daughter is boring compared with my life. I live in a video game, and these people live in the world.

"I'm afraid we're boring you," Sam says.

"Not at all," I say.

"Maybe you thought dinner at the mayor's would be special?" she says.

"To be honest, I was expecting a twenty-one-gun salute between courses."

"Twenty-one guns?" the mayor says. "Is this a chicken dinner or a funeral?"

I laugh.

"Hey, guys, make sure you save room," Sam says.

"Why would we need room?" the mayor says.

"For your surprise," she says.

"You promised me—" the mayor says.

"You know me," she says. "I'm a liar."

"What's going on?" I say.

"It's a special occasion," Sam says.

The mayor shakes his head no, but Sam ignores him.

"It's my father's birthday today," she says.

The mayor covers his face with his hands.

My mind races back to the profile. A birthday in itself might not be critical information, but a birthday that falls directly within the time frame of my assignment? How could I miss that?

"It's true," the mayor says. "I'm a hundred years old today."

"Oh, please," Samara says, nudging her father's arm.

"Okay, I'm fifty-two. But that's closer to a hundred than it is to zero."

"Happy birthday," I say.

"You two stay here and finish," Sam says. "I'll just be a couple minutes."

She kisses the top of her father's head and leaves.

I look at the mayor sitting across from me.

A couple of minutes. That probably means five.

I picture the layout of the apartment, the four players and their locations.

The Pro just finished a walk-through, so he's most likely back in the front vestibule. Sam is in the kitchen twenty feet away from us through a swinging door that creaks on its hinges.

That leaves the mayor. And me.

The mayor stands up.

"Seventh-inning stretch," he says.

"Good idea," I say. I stand and stretch, too, emulating him. I use the motion to complete a full scan of the room.

We're alone.

"I'm glad we have a minute together," he says. "I want to continue our conversation from last night."

The mayor steps toward me, close enough that I can smell his aftershave. It is a pleasant smell. Clean and warm. Like a father should smell.

My father.

A wave of vertigo hits me and the room starts to spin. I jam my thumbs into my eyes.

"Ben?" the mayor says.

"Yes, sir."

"I said I need your help with something."

"My help?"

I take my thumbs from my eyes.

"Let's talk in here," the mayor says, and gestures toward the living room with a conspiratorial flourish.

I let him walk away, and I take a big slug of water.

I breathe. I focus my thoughts.

I see myself as if from above, my position in the room, the apartment, the city block. Then I trace a pathway from me to the mayor, to the place on his skin where I will strike, and back out again.

Out of this apartment, out of the neighborhood, the city, away.

It takes only a second. When I have it mapped in my head, I follow the mayor into the living room.

He is in his favorite pose, looking out the window, lost in thought. He reaches into his pocket and pulls out a small silver case. He takes out a cigarette and jiggles it between his fingers.

He says, "I supposedly gave up smoking during my last campaign. If the press finds out, they'll have my ass. And my daughter will have whatever is left after they're done."

"Your secret is safe with me," I say.

He cracks the window, lights the cigarette, and takes a long pull.

"I'm worried about Sam," he says.

"Worried?"

"There are a lot of changes coming. She's not good with change."

He looks at me for a few seconds, then settles down in an armchair. He opens the bottom drawer of a mahogany cabinet and pulls out an ashtray.

"Sit, Ben."

I do. On the corner of the sofa next to him. Our legs are at a forty-five-degree angle, approximately twenty inches away from each other. When he reaches for the ashtray, he reaches toward me.

"I know Sam trusts you," the mayor says.

I could agree with him, let him say what he's going to say. But this is a smart man. I need to keep that in mind.

The best way to do that is to stick to the truth.

Most of the truth.

I say, "To be honest with you, we just met. I don't know her very well."

"The fact remains that you're here. She's never invited anyone to family dinner before."

"Actually, I invited myself."

The mayor chuckles. "Is that what you think?"

"What do you mean?"

"She asked me this morning if she could invite you."

"She did?"

"She's a crafty one, Ben. She'll keep you on your toes."

I think about the moment in the hall when I suggested Sam invite me to dinner. Was she stage-managing the whole thing?

How could I have missed that?

"You know that my final term is up in a few months," the mayor says.

"I've read about it."

I glance toward the kitchen. No movement there.

The mayor says, "I've been offered something—let's say it's something on a much larger playing field."

"A new job?"

"Of sorts. And if I take it, it's going to mean a lot of changes. For Sam especially."

A new job. New security.

It's adding up to something big, and it must be something related to my assignment. But that doesn't matter now. Not when I'm this close to finishing.

"Changes for Sam," I say. "What does that have to do with me?"

"I want you to take care of her."

"She's got a lot of people taking care of her."

"I know she has friends," the mayor says. "I'm talking about something else."

Just then there's a loud *click*, and the room goes black.

"What's happening?" the mayor says.

I shift in the darkness, my body prepping for danger.

"Happy birthday!" Sam calls from the dining room. The kitchen door hinges creak.

"Here it comes," the mayor says. "Embarrassment on a platter."

He quickly stands and stubs out the cigarette. He stashes the ashtray back in the drawer.

The mayor is arm's-length away from me in the dark. I can sense him there, hear his breathing.

He puts his hand out and touches my shoulder. He whispers in my ear.

"We'll talk about this later," he says. "But please keep it between us for now."

Sam walks out in a flickering halo of candlelight, a cake in her hands.

"What a wonderful surprise!" the mayor says.

It's dark on our side of the room. Candlelit on the other. Shadows in between.

Sam begins to sing.

The mayor leads me toward her, his arm draped casually across my shoulders. Our bodies are close together, so close that I could put my arm around him.

I do.

Finish it. Right now.

I reach across his shoulders with my left arm. My watch arm. I could click a button on the side of my watch dial, then press the back of the buckle into the soft skin on the side of his throat.

We are fifteen steps away from Sam.

Take care of her, the mayor said.

But that is not my job.

In fact it is the opposite of my job.

The mayor's sweater is thick, but his neck is bare above it. My arm is on his sweater. I could reach higher. A few inches is all it would take.

Then it would be done, and I would be away from here. From this family and their conversations over dinner, from questions of trust and care and whatever else is going on here.

I would be away and I would be finished.

Ten steps from Sam.

The mayor sings, and I sing, too.

We are arm in arm now, rocking back and forth, singing together.

I could reach higher. Shift my wrist.

He would stumble. I would catch him. Sam and I would stand over him, and one of us would call for help. It would come quickly, but not quickly enough.

Five steps from Sam.

The mayor hugs me tight against him. I only need to shift my arm—

But I don't.

I sing instead. I smile like they smile.

I emulate.

Before I know it, the song is over and the mayor puts his arm down.

I do the same.

He walks toward the cake, his face illuminated by candlelight. I see how he looks at his daughter. I see how he smiles at her and she smiles back.

I should not care that he smiles.

Men smile as they lie.

Jack's father smiled and betrayed his country.

My father smiled and then Mike appeared.

Now the mayor is smiling, and I am here.

Nobody is innocent. That's what I've been taught.

I've also been taught that assignments are simple.

Finish.

That's all I have to do.

The mayor pulls out his camera and takes a picture of the cake for his blog. He shows me the picture. The frosting glows ghost white in the photo.

Finish.

It's all I have to do, but I cannot do it.

The mayor blows out the candles as Sam and I applaud.

"Let's take a picture together," he says. "The three of us. I want to remember this night."

He reaches for me, but I am already moving away from him. I do not want to touch him again. I do not want to smell the way he smells. I don't want to see how he looks at Sam.

"I have to go to the restroom," I say.

I SLIP INTO THE BATHROOM DOWN THE HALL.

I lock the door behind me and splash water on my face. I look at myself in the mirror.

Something's wrong.

My mind is playing tricks on me. I'm thinking about guilt and innocence, when that is not my job.

My phone vibrates, the double vibration that signals a secure call request from Father.

It's his job to think about these things. My job is much easier.

Finish. Then this will be over. You will pass the test.

A second vibration.

I do not take the call. I turn off my phone.

I formulate a plan.

I will offer to do dishes with Sam, get her working in the kitchen, then make an excuse to go back out and spend time with the mayor.

I need him alone for two minutes. Alone and off guard.

I've still got time. It will be at least ten minutes before the Pro comes through again. That's enough.

I will finish, and then I will call Father to let him know that it is done.

I turn off the water. I ready myself.

There's a knock at the bathroom door.

"Benjamin," Sam says, "let me in."

Do not let her in.

I wipe my face.

"Benjamin."

Do not let her in.

I open the door, and she comes in. She closes the door behind her.

"Are you all right?" she says. "You're acting funny."

"I'm fine."

"Why do you look so uncomfortable?"

"Because we're in a bathroom."

"You're a terrible liar," she says.

She leans back against the door. Anger flares inside. Anger at being trapped, at being dissected by this girl.

"I'm not the one who's lying," I say.

"What are you talking about?"

"You asked your father if you could invite me over tonight."

I'm speaking too fast, not thinking first. Not planning my next move.

"My father said that?"

"Why didn't you tell me?"

"I didn't have a chance, Ben. You asked me first, remember? That's not lying."

I think about it, and she's right. She didn't lie.

"Why did you want me here in the first place?" I say.

She steps toward me. I try to slow my heartbeat, but I cannot.

"The truth?" she says.

"Yes."

"Because of Erica. You two are hitting it off. It's pretty obvious."

"So what?" I say.

She pulls at a thread on the edge of her dress.

"Maybe I'm starting to have feelings for you," she says.

I look in her eyes. She's telling the truth.

I'm suddenly in a different place and time. I'm ten years old, walking down the stairs in our house in Rochester. I hear plates clinking in the kitchen. When I walk in, my mother and father are already sitting down and eating breakfast. There's an empty plate waiting for me in front of my seat.

My seat.

I always sat in the chair across from the window that looked out on the backyard. It was my special place at the table.

"What about you?" Sam says.

"What about me?"

"Do you have feelings for me?"

I take a long breath.

"I—" I try to say something, but I can't.

"Why do you have to be so tough?" she says.

I am in danger here.

The thought forces its way to the front of my consciousness. I am in danger, and so is my assignment.

"Here's the thing, Ben. It's sort of terrible timing."

"Why is that?"

"Things are a little complicated right now. With my ex."

"If he's an ex, why is it complicated?"

"We have this on-again, off-again thing. It's been going on for a few years."

"Is it off or on right now?"

"Something in between."

"That does sound complicated."

"I didn't know I was going to meet you," she says. "And even after I did, I didn't think you gave a crap about me."

"Why is that?"

"Because you're hard to read."

"You seem to be doing a pretty good job of it."

"It doesn't feel that way."

She reaches toward me and I flinch. Just the tiniest bit, but enough. She notes it with a gentle smile.

She says, "I think you're tough outside, but you're soft inside."

"And you?"

"I'm soft everywhere," she says.

Her face is inches from mine. The danger zone. If someone is this close to your face, they can harm you. This close, you cannot see their hands. They could be doing anything, preparing anything, holding anything.

She says, "I'm soft once I trust someone. That's what I should have said."

"And you trust me?" I say.

"Starting to."

This is usually the moment in the assignment where my success is guaranteed. I build trust with the mark until I win them over. Then I can act with assurance.

But this is different. Things are happening that I did not plan.

"I think something's wrong with me," I say.

Because my mind is thinking the wrong things. I should be thinking about finishing my assignment, but I'm thinking about the curve of Sam's neck, the corner of her lip, the way her breasts swell against the fabric of her dress. I'm thinking about the way she laughs when we're together.

"Nothing's wrong," she says. "It's the opposite."

She leans toward me, her lips close to mine, close enough that I feel her breath on my face.

"Your dad's going to wonder about us," I say.

"Let him wonder," she says.

I step back quickly.

"Seriously. We should go back in," I say, and I push past her out the bathroom door.

I LIE TO THEM.

"I'm not feeling well," I say.

"Is it my cooking?" Sam says. She tries to laugh, but I can see she's worried.

I brush off her concerns and the mayor's. I refuse his offer of a ride home.

My excuses are weak, but they are enough.

They get me out.

They get me away.

To the street. To fresh air.

Day two is gone, along with the opportunity to finish my assignment, and there's nobody to blame but myself. I let it go, and I do not let opportunities go. It is not in my training.

My training.

I should be moving toward my assignment, but I am moving away.

Even now I watch myself moving past the doormen, through the vestibule, down the street. I am moving past the cleaners and around the corner until I am out of sight of the police box.

I tell myself to go back, but I keep moving forward until I am away from the apartment and these people and the thoughts that confuse me.

I stop in the middle of the sidewalk, and a sensation sweeps over me.

It's been gnawing at me all night, but now it comes full force.

A familiar smell.

A smell like—

My father

was a warm man.

was kind.

was a professor.

My father held me on his lap when he sat at his desk working. I remember the creak of his leather chair, the casters beneath it that would roll loudly over wood floors.

I'd sneak into his office sometimes after school, kneel on the chair even though my mother forbade it. I'd push off from his desk and I would spin in my father's chair, the smell of him all around me, pervading the wood and leather.

I remember the feeling of being in his arms, his voice vibrating through his chest as he talked to me, my head pressed against him.

I smell him now, the warm, clean scent of his aftershave.

I smell him, but he is not here.

A part of her, Sam had said about her mother. *It is enough.*

A part of my father is around me.

But it is not enough.

I have no choice but to—

"LET GO," A WOMAN SHOUTS.

What woman?

The woman down the street.

The woman in a down vest, brown purse on her arm, 180 degrees behind me in front of the fruit stand at the Korean deli.

The woman I did not see.

The woman being pushed by a dark-haired man in a nylon wind jacket.

The man I also did not see.

He stiff-arms her out of his way, and the container in her hands spills, sending a cascade of blueberries across the sidewalk.

He tramples over them on his way forward.

On his way toward me.

I see it now, the trajectory he's on, the fact that I missed him advancing on me from behind.

No matter.

Choices:

Do I go back toward the mayor's with the police box that might neutralize this threat?

Or do I go forward toward the unknown, toward danger, toward potential discovery about the nature of my pursuer?

One second to decide before my retreat is cut off.

I do not need the whole second. I choose forward. Or my body chooses for me.

I start down Columbus Avenue, heading south.

The avenue is nearly deserted this time of night, and it leaves me exposed on an open street. I've got no choice but to keep moving.

Unusual, his methods. If he catches me here, what will he do in public and on the street?

I don't intend to find out. Not on his terms.

I want to be on Broadway, where it's busier and I have more options. When I hit 79th Street, I turn and head west toward the avenue.

That's when I feel it.

The Presence from the other night.

The Presence is somewhere in front of me while the man in the nylon jacket pursues me from behind. That means there are two of them.

And then another man pops out of an alley as I pass by and joins the man behind.

Three of them now.

Maybe my turn at 79th was a mistake. I don't often make mistakes, but maybe the move was too predictable. There's no time to dwell on it.

I adjust and they match me, keeping pace with my zigs and zags.

Three against one. The odds are in their favor.

I feel the faint rumbling of the 1 train coming in beneath my feet. Let's see how good they are in the subway.

DOWN.

Into darkness. Damp concrete stairs and flickering light from below. Two men and the Presence on the street above.

I hit the platform of the local station, and I'm relieved to find it relatively crowded.

People coming from the Amsterdam bars and an event at the museum. More people heading toward late dinner in Midtown.

The rumble in the ground becomes a wind in the tunnel followed by the oncoming rush of a southbound local train.

I slide into the crowd without anybody noticing.

Not quite true. One person notices.

"Are you following me?" Erica says.

She sways on the platform, eyes heavy.

Shit. I do not need this.

"Where did you come from?" I say.

"I was partying with some friends."

I glance at my watch. "The party ended early," I say.

I study her. Red-cheeked, disheveled.

Is this a setup? Is she a part of a trap?

"The party ended early because I took off," she says. "One of the guys got all date-rapey with me."

"Are you okay?"

"Oh, please," she says. "I can handle myself. The son of a bitch is going to be icing his lowboys for a few days."

"Good for you," I say.

Her story sounds right. The location is right, as is her appearance.

It's not a setup. It's a coincidence.

The train pulls in. I sense motion behind me on the platform. The Presence and his two men coming down the staircase. I can't see them, but I feel them closing in.

"Will you take me home, Ben? I have a killer headache."

She leans into me.

Choices.

I could leave her here, but will she be safe?

If I shrug her off fast, the people following me might read it as contact with a drunk stranger. A second longer and they'll think I ran into an acquaintance. Longer still and she'll appear to be someone who matters, someone they can use to get to me.

"Benji, Ben-ben," she says, and kisses my neck.

She just made the choice for us both.

I can't let her go now.

The train doors open and people move toward it, the platform emptying quickly.

Movement in my peripheral vision. The pursuers making their move.

The train chimes, warning of its departure.

"Stand clear of the closing doors," a voice barks.

I wait.

I need the pursuers closer. I need them to wonder which way I will go.

I move like I don't know they're here, like I think I lost them with my dodge into the subway. I hesitate, my body swaying between options. I want them confused about me and my skill level. I might be good enough to know they're here, but not good enough to know what to do about it.

That is what I make my body tell them.

"We're going to miss the train," Erica whines.

"We won't miss it," I say. "I guarantee."

At the last second, I put an arm around her and pull her into the train car, and the doors close behind us.

A second later a man's face hits the glass, his fingers caught between the closed doors.

Speakers blare. The train attendant shouts at the guy.

His fingers stay there.

I watch him over Erica's shoulder. I log details.

Olive skin. Unshaven. The collar of his wind jacket askew.

I think of the man speaking Arabic yesterday. The new clothes he was wearing. This man is similar, but he's not the Presence.

The conductor doesn't want to open the door for this guy. It happens from time to time. Stubborn rider. More stubborn conductor. Standoff.

Usually the rider gives. It's not like he wants to lose his arm.

But it's not like they can drag him down the tunnel, either.

The battle goes for ten seconds, long enough for passengers to start to groan.

I'm trying to make sense of what I'm seeing. Windbreaker is in public with witnesses all around, but he continues to push toward me, not caring.

The conductor finally relents. The bell chimes, and the doors open.

"Tell me something," Erica says.

"Anything," I say.

Windbreaker steps into our subway car. The doors close behind him.

"If you had to choose between me and Sam, who would you choose?"

"What am I choosing you for?" I say.

"You know," she says.

Windbreaker turns toward me.

I pull Erica with me to the rear of the car.

"Where are we going? I want to sit down, already," she whines.

"We will."

Windbreaker advances. But he moves slowly, not at all like someone who wants to catch up to us.

Interesting.

If he's not trying to catch us, what is he doing?

Herding.

I recognize it now. Three men moving in tandem. This is a tactic, a variation of the pincer movement. It's an attack from the front obscuring a flanking maneuver.

A military tactic.

This means the real danger is not in front but behind. In the car attached to ours.

As Windbreaker comes forward, the natural response is to retreat and transfer to another car to get away. You think you are escaping danger, but you are walking into it.

What is the unnatural response?

Go toward him.

"I see a seat down at the other end," I say.

I take Erica with me toward Windbreaker. His eyes narrow. I am not following his plan.

The train accelerates away from the station, rocking side to side.

I head directly for Windbreaker, one arm around Erica.

Windbreaker reaches into his pocket.

Maximum danger in five seconds.

"Jerry!" I shout at him. The first name that comes into my head.

I lunge forward, Erica held tightly at my side. I reach for Windbreaker like I'm reaching to hug a friend. I grasp him before he can react, a crushing hug that pins his arms hard against his side and keeps his hand from leaving his pocket.

As the train lurches and the brakes squeal, I slam his head hard into the metal pole at the same time. The *crack* is lost in the sound of the brakes. I follow through with the motion, swinging him around and dropping him into the open seat.

Then I turn and slide open the door between subway cars, hanging on to Erica the whole time.

A brief scream of brakes and wind as we step out onto the exposed metal platforms swinging between cars, navigate across the gap, and slam open the door, passing through to the safety of the next car.

"What was that?" she says. "Did you know that guy?"

"I thought I did. I was wrong."

I notice an empty seat by the door.

"You want to sit now?" I say.

"If you're done dragging me around, mister."

"Done. I promise."

"I'm so wasted," she says. "I have to cut down on my partying."

She flops down, head in hands.

I sense movement in the car we were just in. Windbreaker is out of commission, so man number two is coming forward. He's wearing a light spring jacket and bright white, perfectly clean sneakers. Too clean.

"Are you okay for a second?" I say to Erica.

The train rocks. This conductor is a real cowboy. He's helping me without knowing it.

"Where are you going?" she says, starting to nod out.

"I forgot something," I say.

"You never answered the question about me and Sam," she says.

"I have to think about it," I say.

"You shouldn't have to think about a question like that."

I watch Sneakers coming forward. He reaches for the subway door in the car next to ours. Left hand on the door handle, right hand going into his jacket pocket.

I wait for him to open the door to his car, then I open mine.

We meet in the middle.

Roaring wind. Darkness.

A flurry of blows. Most of them glance off my side. He's good. He's fast.

I am faster.

Four blows rising from waist to head.

The train screams around a bend. Centrifugal force pulls him back and me forward. I use the inertia to straight-arm him in the chest. He reels back on the tiny landing. The guard chain snaps, and he swings out into the darkness.

Brakes squeal.

I reach for him.

He teeters on one leg, reaching back toward me, trying to stop his fall. I grasp the corner of his jacket, trying to pull him back. It slips between my fingers, and I grasp tighter.

There is no need for this man to die now. I need him disabled. I need to ask him some questions.

The noise in the tunnel doubles. On the other track, a train roars forward.

Timing.

A single hard yank to get him back. It should work.

It does not.

The jacket slips, his eyes widen in fear, his fingers claw at my face—

And then he's gone, his body bouncing like a limp doll from train to train before being sucked beneath the rushing metal on the opposite track.

I stand alone in the space between cars with his jacket in my hands. There are no shouts from inside the car, no emergency brake pulled.

Nothing at all.

It happened too quickly.

Sneakers is gone, and that leaves only one man.

The Presence.

I glance behind me to check on Erica. She's dozing on the bench, her chin on her chest. So I move away from her into the other car.

Toward the Presence.

I run through the car. Eyes look up at me, then back down. It's a New York subway. You notice everything, but you don't see anything at all.

I make it to the end of the car as we pull into the 72nd Street station.

I note movement a car away. The Presence.

He looks back at me. A quick look, but enough.

I see his face for the first time.

Dark complexion, curly black hair, and a well-trimmed beard.

I've seen this man before.

Faces flip like playing cards through my mind. They move faster and faster until they stop on—

The Apple Store.

I saw this man in the Apple Store on my first day in New York when I was buying my phone. That means he was the one who followed me afterward.

He's been on me from the beginning, nearly from the time I arrived in the city.

That's not precise. He might have been on me when I arrived, but I did not see him until later. After I entered school.

After I met Sam.

It's a tenuous connection, maybe even coincidental. I met Sam, and then I was followed.

There are other scenarios that might explain the Presence, but I can't know what they are without more information.

The quickest way to get information is to catch him.

That's what I'm going to do.

Now.

I rush forward as the train grinds to a stop, racing directly at the Presence.

The doors open, and he leaps out of the car to get away from me, pushing past the riders who block his path. I jump out of my own car onto a platform filled with people.

I look everywhere trying to reacquire him, but I cannot.

The Presence is gone, swallowed up by the crowd. And with him, my opportunity.

I walk slowly down the platform and get back onto the car where Erica is sleeping.

Passengers stream in. I squeeze in next to her.

She stirs. "I'm cold, Benjamin."

She tugs at the jacket in my hands. The one that belonged to Sneakers. I put it on her.

"Mmm. Cozy," she says.

I run my hands through the pockets, checking for the weapon. It's gone.

"Are you searching me?" Erica mumbles.

"I'm looking for my ChapStick," I say.

"Keep looking," she says. "It feels nice."

I stop looking.

She sighs, reaches into the breast pocket, comes out with a price tag.

"No ChapStick. Sorry," she says.

She hands me the tag.

Brand-new, from Gap. Just like the man I killed in the town house.

Men with military training come to the United States, they're in a rush, and they want to fit in. What do they do?

"Funny. You're not really a Gap guy," Erica says.

"I'm a lot of different things," I say.

They disguise themselves, posing as something they are not. Just like me.

It cannot be a coincidence. We are moving toward the same finish line but with different objectives. I am aimed at the mayor, and they are aimed at me.

Why?

Five days, two of them gone. Three left.

What's happening three days from now?

Erica pulls the jacket tight around her. She lays her head on my shoulder, and her soft hair brushes against my cheek.

"I feel safe with you," she says.

And she drifts off to sleep.

I make sure she gets home okay, then I make sure I do.

"YOU'RE KILLING ME," HOWARD SAYS.

Friday morning. Day 3. The school hallway.

Howard's sentence comes out as a squeal, the words barely comprehensible. But I comprehend because I've heard words like these before. They are the words of someone begging for his life.

Howard comes into view, trapped in yet another corner of the school hall by Justin and his greasy-faced friend. Justin is pushing Howard into the wall, squashing him with a beanbag chair.

Howard is trapped.

The idea causes something uncomfortable to stir inside me.

"I can't breathe," Howard says.

I glance over again. Justin isn't really going to kill Howard, just make his life hell until he does it himself.

It's got nothing to do with me. That's what I tell myself.

Guys like Howard live like this. It's their burden to bear. They don't get to make choices about who they want to be in the world.

The choice is already made for them, maybe from birth, maybe from bad luck. Who knows?

They only have to live with the consequences. Or invent the next Facebook and get their revenge.

In any case, it's none of my business. So I keep walking.

Justin steps back like he's letting Howard go, then he jumps forward into the beanbag. Howard's head smacks against the wall with a loud thump.

Sam's not around. Nobody's around.

Except me.

Goddamn it.

I turn and head toward them.

"What's up," I say, loud enough to be heard down the hall.

Justin's head pivots toward me, but he doesn't stop pushing. His greasy friend steps out to block my path.

"Mind your own business," the guy says.

"I should," I say. "I really should. But I'm not going to."

Greasy chuckles. A drop of spittle flies from his lips.

He's about a minute from drinking through a straw for the next six weeks.

But I don't want to hurt anyone. Not if I don't have to.

Choices.

I'll try to play peacemaker. Start with the least aggressive posture.

"Let's call it a day, guys. What do you say?"

"What do you say?" Greasy parrots me.

Wrong move.

"Straw or crutches," I ask him.

"What's that?"

"It's how you're going to live for the next six weeks. I'm giving you a choice."

He laughs. "What's the straw?" he says.

"Forget I mentioned it," I say.

I break his ankle.

Not break. Dislocate.

I do it in one motion. I bring my heel down at a certain angle, let gravity and weight do most of the work. He drops like a demolished building and bursts into tears.

"What the hell—" Justin says.

He barely has time to get the words out before I've sideswiped him, knocking him off Howard and down to the floor.

It's a layer cake. Ground on the bottom. Then beanbag. Then Justin. Then me with a knee in Justin's back.

"You're going to leave Howard alone," I say.

"Like hell," Justin says. "He's a freak. You don't know the story."

"What sport do you play?" I say.

"Soccer," he says.

I'm feeling magnanimous, so I leave his feet alone.

I break his wrist.

Not break. Hyperextend.

"Fuuuck—" he cries out, rolling onto his side and clutching his injured paw.

Howard watches, mouth open in surprise.

"Now we walk away," I say to Howard.

"What about these guys?" he says.

"They were roughhousing and it went too far. Right, guys?"

Justin groans and nods. Greasy is still crying.

"Don't worry," I say. "They can fix you up in the emergency room."

Their injuries are consistent with a wrestling match that got out of hand. I made sure of it.

I lead Howard away.

"Why did you help me?" he says.

I'm wondering the same thing. Why would I choose to expose myself in this way? In any way?

Stupid. Damn stupid. But it felt good, too. That's the part I'm having trouble understanding.

"I don't know," I say to Howard.

Which is the truth. There are too many things like this lately. Things I do without knowing why, motivations that I cannot fully comprehend.

"Whatever the reason, I owe you," Howard says.

We turn into the main hallway. I watch how students pass to either side of us, not wanting to get too close to Howard. He's got an eighteen-inch exclusion zone around him at all times.

"You've got a lot of enemies," I say.

"A whole school of them," he says.

"What did you do?"

"I'm weird."

"Lots of people are weird, but they're not hated by everyone in school. What story is Justin talking about?"

"I got caught doing some things...." Howard says, his voice trailing off.

"What did you do, Howard?"

"I was playing with myself, okay? In the library. Back in ninth grade."

He looks at the ground.

"That's embarrassing," I say, "but you can't be the first guy to look for a happy ending in the library."

"If I tell you the whole thing, you might never talk to me again."

"I'm the guy who got thrown out of Choate, remember?"

Howard nods.

"I was using a book when they caught me," he says.

"Reading a book?"

"No, rubbing myself with one. *The Sound and the Fury*."

"You were masturbating with Faulkner?"

"I love the classics."

I have to stifle a laugh.

"They went through the stacks after that. Most of the pages of the senior reading list were stuck together."

"I'm surprised you're still in school."

"I got suspended. Psych eval and everything. The doctor said I was acting out my disdain for the educational system."

"What do you say?"

"I say the seniors are assholes. Anyway, the administration let me come back with mandatory psychological monitoring. The paperwork said I had a mental breakdown because of bullying. You use the word *bullying* these days, you pretty much write your own ticket."

"So you got to stay in school."

"It was the biggest mistake I ever made," he says, gesturing to the halls. "I thought people would forget eventually, but they didn't."

"Some mistakes are like that," I say.

"Like what?" Howard says.

I think of my first day in the training house, Mother looking at me across her desk.

"Permanent," I say.

Howard stops.

"Since we're being honest with each other, can I tell you something?" he says.

I nod. He steps closer and his voice drops to a whisper.

"I know you're not a student," he says.

"I'm not?"

I study Howard's face. He looks scared.

"Not like the rest of us," he says.

I put a hand on his chest and push him through the men's room door.

THE BATHROOM IS EMPTY.

I keep pushing Howard until I back him up to the wall. I hold him there by the fabric of his shirt.

"What are you saying, Howard?"

"I don't think you were at Choate," he says. "Or if you were, it wasn't to study."

"What else would I be doing there?"

"Killing people."

I can finish this in fifteen seconds. Pressure on Howard's carotid artery, not enough to cause bruising.

"Why would I kill people?" I say.

"Because you're a vampire," Howard says.

I stop, let go of his shirt.

"A vampire?"

"I've been watching you," Howard says. "You're quiet. You have strange energy. You sort of disappear sometimes. And you're stronger than everyone else. You kicked those guys' asses like it was nothing."

I knew that was a mistake.

"There's no such thing as vampires," I say.

"It's okay with me if you are. Just please make me one, too, Ben. I'll be a weak vampire. That's okay with me. As long as I'm stronger than those guys so I can defend myself."

"This conversation is over," I say.

I head for the bathroom door.

"Don't leave me in this school!" he says.

I stop and rub my forehead, frustrated.

He says, "You know what's going to happen. Those guys are going to wait for you to leave school, and then they'll kill me as payback. You won't be here to protect me."

"There's nothing I can do about that," I say.

"You can take me with you."

This is why I don't connect with people. They are complicated. They want things from me, things I can't give.

"I hate it here," Howard says. "I have no life."

"It gets better," I say. "Haven't you seen those videos?"

Does it get better? For Howard? For me?

I can't be sure.

"I can be useful to you," Howard says. "Do you need money?"

"I've got plenty of money."

"I can make sure you get straight A's."

"I don't need A's. Howard, how can you do all this stuff?"

"I told you, I'm good with computers."

I think of Howard in front of the computer yesterday, his

fingers moving at blazing speed. I thought he was just a lonely kid with computer chops. But he's more than that.

"You really are a hacker. "

He nods. "I can get into sites. I can erase your identity and create a new one."

That troubles me. I'm not sure how elaborate my cover is online. For normal searches it's fine, but could it withstand serious scrutiny from an obsessive kid with upper-level hacking skills?

Howard is dangerous to me.

Or useful.

I think about last night, my inaction around the mayor, my wondering about guilt and innocence.

What if I could prove that the mayor is guilty?

Then I would understand why I was sent here, and whatever is happening with Sam wouldn't matter so much. My hesitation would disappear.

The problem: It's forbidden to ask why I was sent.

I cannot reach out to The Program for information of this sort. The only option is to go rogue, to find the information I want on my own.

But that would betray every principle of my training.

I will not do it.

My phone vibrates with a secure text notification from Father. Three numeric signs:

It looks like someone slipped and pressed a key too many times, but in fact it's code. An order for an immediate and mandatory check-in.

I didn't call him back last night, because I was stalling for time. I thought I'd be done by now, and I'd have good news to report.

Unfortunately that's not the case.

"We have to talk about this another time," I tell Howard.

I move him toward the door.

"So you're going to think about taking me with you?" he says.

"I'll think about it."

Anything to get him out the door.

"I owe you one, Ben. I won't forget that."

I get him outside and lock the door behind him.

Then I call Father and I wait for the line to go live.

"You didn't return my calls last night," he says.

"I've been busy, Dad. Sorry."

"Good busy or bad busy?"

"I'm at school, so I can't get into it."

"I know where you are," he says.

How does he know?

I glance at the stall doors. There's nobody in here. I look at the ceiling and along the molding, searching for drill markings or camera pinholes.

Father says, "I know where you are now, and I know where you were last night. You were having a good time when you should have been doing your homework."

"That's not what happened."

"Then tell me what's preventing you from handing in your assignment."

"Complications."

Sam is a complication.

No, my reaction to Sam is the complication. And my reaction to her father.

"I need a little more time," I say.

"About that. There's been a change. Your assignment has to be turned in by tomorrow."

Tomorrow?

That's four days instead of five.

"I don't understand."

"It's not up for discussion," Father says. "I got the message, and I'm passing it along to you. Do we understand each other?"

"Completely."

"Should I expect more complications?"

Silence hangs in the digital space between us.

I make my voice cold, professional.

"No complications," I say.

"That's what I wanted to hear," he says, and he ends the call.

Tomorrow.

That means I have only one more day to get to the mayor and finish my assignment.

That's a disturbing thought, but it's followed by an even more disturbing one:

One last day to finish means I have only one more day with Sam.

I AM RUNNING FAST.

It's the track-and-field rotation in phys ed, and a few students have persuaded the teacher to let us run outside. Sam and Erica are up ahead of me, leading the class. Erica is in first position, her legs short and powerful like a gymnast's. Sam is a couple of paces back, her strides longer, her build narrow and beautiful. I watch her hair bouncing in a ponytail across her shoulders as she runs.

One more day with Sam.

She glances back at me, but I avoid meeting her eye.

We haven't spoken since I ran from the mayor's penthouse last night. I noticed myself shying from her in class, my body turning away as hers turned toward. Even now, I look down rather than meet her eye.

I don't know this person, the one who avoids a girl because he doesn't know what to say to her. I don't know the guy who is distracted, who worries, who takes chances that are not strictly necessary.

Sam glances back again from the front of the pack.

She has questions. It's obvious.

I have questions, too. Different questions.

For now, I run through Central Park, grateful to be in motion. I would run harder if I could, run past all these people, run until the doubts disappeared and I felt like myself again.

"You think you'll win the Asshole 10K again this year?"

It's Darius. He plods up beside me, sneakers slapping on pavement.

"Give it a rest," I say.

"No, I'm not going to give it a rest. You think you can give me a drink at a party, and that's a free pass to chase after our women?"

He looks at Sam and Erica up ahead.

"What's with you, Darius? You've been on my back since day one."

"Do you know how many guys I've watched take a shot at Sam?"

"Why don't you take a shot and join the club? You'll feel better about yourself."

His face goes red.

He says, "If you cared about her, you'd leave her alone."

I look at him. He's serious.

"Why does she need to be left alone?"

"I'm not telling you."

"Tell me something. Help me understand."

I play like I'm on his side in this thing, like we can find a way to deal together.

"You're making her life more complicated than it already is."

"Why is it complicated?"

"Because of that Israeli asshole."

"What are you guys talking about?" Sam says.

She's dropped back to our position.

I glance at Darius. He warns me off with a subtle head shake.

"What guys always talk about," I say.

"You mean sports," she says. "And your crotches."

"Two for two," I say.

Erica notices us behind her and drops back, too. "Did you guys get interrogated by the administration yet?" she says.

"What for?" I say.

"Didn't you hear? Justin and his boy got into it in the hall today and messed each other up. They're asking if anyone saw anything."

"I saw the whole thing," I say.

"Really?" Erica says.

"More than saw. I'm the guy who kicked both their asses."

The girls burst out laughing.

"Like hell," Darius says.

He side-checks me, shifting in midstride and slamming me with his hip. Nothing too hard. Just enough to make his point.

I stumble like he knocked me off balance.

"Yeah, you're a real badass," he says.

He laughs and runs ahead. Erica looks from Sam to me.

"Wait up, Darius," she says, and she runs up to join him.

Now it's Sam and me, running together near the back of the pack.

"Am I allowed to run next to you, or am I still getting the silent treatment?" Sam says.

"Can you run quietly?" I say.

She smiles.

"What happened to you last night, Ben?"

"I felt sick. I think it was something I ate."

I hope to get a laugh and distract her, but it doesn't work.

"I don't believe that," she says. "I think you ran away."

"Why would I run?"

"That's what I'm trying to figure out."

The phys ed teacher passes us. She says, "Stay together, okay? I don't want to lose anyone in the park."

We wave to her, and she runs on.

"I'm getting tired," Sam says.

I look at her legs, toned from regular exercise. There's no way she's tired from this little run. She slows, and I slow to keep pace with her. Now we're dead last in the pack.

"I've got a cramp or something—" Sam says.

She limps for a few steps, then stops. The rest of the class continues on.

"Anything I can do?" I say.

"You can try to keep up," she says, and she darts down a side path and disappears from sight.

So much for the cramp.

I take off after her.

THE TREES ARE A BLUR ON EITHER SIDE OF US.

Sam is quick, much quicker than I expected. She cuts from the side path to a dirt path and then into the woods, all without telegraphing a move. I can barely keep up with her.

It's not that she's faster than me. She simply knows this place better. Home-court advantage, so to speak. She moves in directions I don't expect, down paths that I can't see until I'm nearly past them. I catch brief glimpses of her running between trees.

Brief glimpses, and then nothing.

Because she has disappeared.

I stop and listen to her footfalls receding in the forest, trying to determine which way to go. I hear something off to my left where the trees are so dense that the sunlight is blocked out.

I hesitate for a moment, and then I step off the path.

I wind my way through the trees, pausing to listen for Sam every few steps.

There is no sound but distant traffic outside the park.

I stop and look around.

I'm lost.

I consider turning back, but instead I stay where I am. I project my energy outward.

I sense her off to my left.

I move in that direction and pop through a thicket of trees into a clearing. There's a statue in front of me, a giant stone obelisk that comes to a point at the top.

Sam waits by it, smiling and breathless.

"You found me," she says. "I'm impressed."

"What was that all about?"

"You've been running away from me all day," she says. "I wanted to reverse the direction."

"Why would you want that?"

"Come on, Ben. What really happened last night?"

"I was confused."

"About what?"

I think of Sam and me in the bathroom last night, her lips inches from mine.

"My feelings," I say.

She smiles.

"You do have feelings for me."

I turn away from her. I walk around the deserted plaza, examining the statue, giving myself some breathing room.

"What is this place?" I say.

"It's called Cleopatra's Needle," she says.

I look at the statue behind her, the green-black stone rising into the sky.

"It's the oldest statue in the park," she says. "The oldest in New York, I think."

"What's written on it?"

"Egyptian hieroglyphs. It's called Cleopatra's Needle, but it has nothing to do with Cleopatra. It was created a thousand years before her reign. I come here sometimes when I need to think. It's my private place."

"Now I know about it."

"You know all my private places," she says with a grin.

"Not yet I don't."

I walk around the obelisk. The stone is crumbling, the glyphs fading from exposure to the elements.

Sam says, "I have dual citizenship, did you know that? Maybe that's why I like the statue. Something so foreign plopped down in the middle of the city. Kind of like me."

The sky has darkened, and a wind is starting to blow. She comes and stands beside me.

"Do you ever wonder where you belong?" she says. "Like maybe life made a mistake and put you someplace you weren't supposed to be?"

I think of my real parents. My first life.

"Sometimes I think about that," I say.

Between assignments. Never during.

Never before now.

She stares at the statue, lost in thought.

"For a while I was scared that you and Erica were a match, but the more I get to know you, the more I don't think so."

I want to ask her more, but I stop myself. I have only one day, and I keep getting distracted by these conversations.

I need to surprise Sam right now, change the focus of the conversation. Back to her father. To the future.

There's something big brewing, and I need to know what it is.

"Your father told me everything," I say.

Sam stops walking and looks back at me.

I'm bluffing, but she doesn't know that.

"Why would he tell you?" she says.

"Because he's worried about you."

That part is true. I don't know why he's worried, but I'm guessing Sam does.

"They asked him to be Special Envoy for Middle East Peace," she says.

She slumps down at the base of the statue.

I think about the Presence, the Arabic spoken by his man. Is it possible the mayor is working with them in some way? Is this why they're after me?

"Did he say yes?" I ask.

"Not yet. He's weighing options. I told him he should just go back to his company, but he says he's made enough money for ten lifetimes. He wants to stay in public service."

"It sounds like the envoy position will let him do that."

"And ruin my life at the same time."

"How will it ruin your life?"

"Bad things happened in Israel, Ben. I don't want to go back there."

A drop of rain hits my forehead.

"It's starting to rain," she says. "We should get back to school."

She looks at the sky. It's overcast now, and the wind is gusting.

"Or—where do you live?" she says.

"98th Street," I say.

"School's closer."

"It is," I say as the drops become a steady drizzle. "But we're going to get wet either way."

"Are you inviting me to your place?"

"Sounds like it," I say, and I take off running.

For a second I worry that she won't follow me. But then I hear her footsteps splashing behind me. She catches up to me a second later.

"You're not going to get away this time," she says.

"I wasn't trying to get away," I say.

We run together through the rain, leaping across puddles and dodging traffic as we make our way uptown.

SAM TOWELS OFF HER HAIR IN MY LIVING ROOM.

"I'm soaked through," she says. "Do you have a robe or something?"

I look at her standing there, wet clothes pasted to her body.

"Hello?" she says.

"Sorry. Let me grab something."

I don't know if I have a robe, but I check the closet in the bedroom, and I find one hanging on a hook on the wall. The Program thinks of everything.

Not everything. They weren't thinking about this when they left me a robe.

I go back into the living room to find the gas fireplace lit. Sam is drying off in front of it.

"I'm freezing," she says.

She grabs the robe from me.

"Turn around," she says.

"The bathroom is right—"

"I don't need the bathroom," she says.

She gestures with her finger for me to turn around.

I turn toward the wall as Sam gets undressed behind me.

"I've been thinking about the first day in AP European," I say over my shoulder.

"That was a long time ago."

"Only three days."

"It seems like ten years."

I hear wet clothes hitting the floor.

"What were you thinking?" Sam says.

"I was wondering why you spoke to me after class that day."

"There was something about you. I wanted to know who you were."

"Do you want to know who every new student is?"

"Only the cute ones," she says. "You can turn around now."

I turn and Sam strikes a pose. She is wearing the robe cinched tightly in the middle, her hair slicked back, her legs bare.

"What do you think?" she says.

"I think you should wear more robes."

She laughs. The flames flicker at her feet.

She walks around the living room. She touches one of the photos on the end table.

"You said you didn't have a lot of photos," she says.

"I have a few."

"Are these your parents?" she says.

"Supposedly. I never see them."

"Lucky you."

"I thought you were pro-parent."

"I fooled you."

"But you have a great relationship with your father."

"I do. In public."

"In private, too. I've seen you."

"If you saw us, it wasn't private, was it? You think that just because you're in a politician's house, you're seeing the real person? Pretty naive, Ben."

"You sound angry."

"Yeah, well. I have my reasons."

She puts a smile on her face, but it's like she's putting on a mask. I've seen this before with people in the public eye. Real emotions, quickly covered by fake ones.

And I've seen it in myself. It's what I've been trained to do.

She touches the photo of my parents one last time, then continues around the apartment.

"Your place barely looks lived in," she says.

"We have a great cleaning service. And I'm not home much."

"Poor Benjamin. It must be hard being trapped all alone in a big apartment."

"I'm not trapped," I say.

"We're both trapped in lives we didn't choose."

"Speak for yourself."

I watch her moving around the room, examining things.

I don't like how much focus she's giving the place, almost like she's investigating. Is this what it feels like when a girl is in your space for the first time?

"I know all about your life," she says.

"What do you know?"

I watch her face in the flickering firelight, monitoring it for signs of dangerous intent.

"I know you're trapped by the system," she says. "You're trapped by this country and the way you think about it. You're trapped by being a teenager, and—I haven't met your parents, but if they're sending you to a school like ours, you're trapped in their expectations of you."

"It's not true," I say.

"Tell me one thing you've ever done, one decision you've ever made on your own."

Unlike a normal teenager, I make all my own decisions. Nobody tells me what to eat, when to go to bed, what I can or can't do on the weekend. I don't have family to answer to, kid brothers to take care of, relatives to call on their birthdays. I don't have to worry about grades or getting into college or what I'm going to do when I get older. I am completely free day to day.

But on a larger scale, everything I do is an assignment. My life is dictated by The Program.

The more I think about it, what looks like freedom is really the opposite. My life has never been my own, not since the day Mike arrived at school.

"I see you thinking about it, and you know I'm right, don't you?" Sam says. "You've never made a decision for yourself."

That's when it hits me.

"There's one decision I've made on my own," I say.

"Tell me."

"My decision to kiss you."

That stops her. But only for a second.

"When did you decide that?" she says.

"Just now."

"Oh really? Do I get a vote in the matter?"

"You voted yes," I say, and I step in and kiss her, a long, slow first kiss that makes my skin tingle.

"Wow," she says. "If that's your idea of democracy, I'm a believer."

She pulls me back in for a second kiss, more passionate than the first.

We come up for air, our bodies still pressed together.

I look into Sam's eyes, and suddenly I'm thinking about the first girl, the girl from the convenience store. The one with blue eyes.

You're going to think you love me after this, she said. *But you'll be wrong.*

"Benjamin."

Sam whispers a name. For a moment I don't know who she's talking to, and then I remember.

My name. My assignment.

Sam is in my arms now, her body warm against mine, her lips so close that we share a breath.

"You went away for a second," she says.

"I'm afraid to get close to you," I say.

It pops out of me, a thought I would never share with anyone.

Sam runs her fingers through my hair.

"I'm glad you told me that," she says. "I'm afraid, too."

"Why are you afraid?"

"You first," she says.

"There's a lot about me you don't know," I say. "Who I am. The reasons I'm in New York."

"I know more than you think," she says.

"What do you know?"

She touches my chest.

"I know what's in here," she says. "Maybe nothing else matters."

I think about that for a second. I wish it were true, but I don't think it is.

"What about you?" I say. "Why are you afraid?"

"I don't want to hurt you."

"How could you hurt me?"

"It's happened before."

I think of the *Daily News* headline that Howard showed me.

"Did you hurt someone?" I say.

She nods.

"Intentionally?"

"No," she says.

"Then maybe it doesn't matter."

"Nothing matters tonight. Is that what we're saying?"

"I think it is."

She touches my face, gently tracing my lips with her finger.

"When are your parents coming back?" she says.

"They're out of town."

"That's convenient."

"Isn't it?"

She opens the robe, and in an instant my doubts about her are forgotten, along with my concerns about the mayor, the assignment, The Program.

Sam's right. Nothing matters tonight.

Only us.

THE STORM HAS ALMOST PASSED.

A light drizzle falls, reflecting lights up and down the avenue.

Sam and I walk hand in hand. We stay close, tucked under the same umbrella.

Along the avenue, a horn honks, followed by the squeal of brakes.

A doorman pops out of a building, an unlit cigarette already in his mouth.

A cab splashes through a puddle and we jump back. On the cab roof:

Home is where the ♥ is.

I think of home.

Not a faraway home. Not the home of my past, or the home of some imagined future.

Not the home I had with The Program.

Here. Now. With Sam.

Sam feels like home.

A flash of light in my eyes snaps me back to reality.

Sam is holding a camera phone. She's just taken a picture of me.

"What are you doing?" I say.

I try to keep my voice controlled, but I hear my volume increase.

"Do you hate cameras that much?" she says.

"I'm not photogenic," I say.

She looks at her phone screen.

"Yeah, you look like crap," she says. "Bedhead."

I could grab the phone away from her. I could demand that she delete it. I could tell her it really bothers me, that I've been burned by an ex-girlfriend and I don't want it to happen again.

I could raise a host of objections, but that might seem strange.

"Why do you want a picture of me?" I say.

"I'm going to be thinking about you all night. I wanted something to look at while I do. Is that okay?"

"I guess so."

"Do you want to take a picture of me? Reciprocity and all that?"

"No."

"You don't want a picture?" she says, getting upset.

"I have a picture," I say. I point to my head. "In here. No delete button."

"That is uncharacteristically romantic of you."

"I have my moments."

She puts her phone away.

"I saw your scar," she says. "Before, when you took your shirt off."

My hand automatically goes to my chest.

The knife wound. I think of Mike, and it makes me angry, his face intruding at this moment, his mark forever branded on my skin.

"It's no big deal," I say.

"How did it happen?"

A flicker of fear crosses her face. Is she simply curious, or is there something else? I sense her back away slightly.

"I had a car accident when I was a kid," I say. "They did some surgery."

"On your heart?"

"It missed the heart. Just barely."

"Is it painful?"

"Not anymore," I say.

She puts a hand on my chest where the scar is, but I don't feel it. The skin is dead there.

"Poor Benjamin," she says, and she moves closer.

We kiss in the shadows beneath a building overhang a few blocks from the mayor's residence.

Her phone vibrates in her purse. She breaks off the kiss.

"I have to check this real quick."

She looks at her phone, and her expression changes. She suddenly looks serious.

"It's getting late," she says. "I'd better get home."

The assignment comes rushing back.

One day. That's all I have left.

"What are you doing tomorrow?" I say.

"My dad needs my help with something," she says. "It's going to be a busy weekend, actually. I probably can't see you until Monday."

I'll think about this moment in the days to come, the way she looks over my shoulder as she says it when she should be looking in my eyes.

I'll wonder whether I should have challenged her, forced the issue in some way.

But in the moment, I don't do any of those things.

"I understand," I say.

"I'll call if I can," she says.

I stroke her hair once, then feel it pass through my fingers as she turns and heads for home.

She's ten yards away when my phone vibrates.

A double vibration, repeated twice.

The Poker app. I've been dealt a hand.

It's Mother.

I play the hand and the line connects.

"Go home," Mother says.

The line cuts off.

MOTHER DOES NOT CALL DURING AN ASSIGNMENT.

Never before this.

I've made a terrible mistake.

Sleeping with Sam, opening up my life to her. Revealing myself on any level.

I've made a terrible mistake, and now I'm caught.

The thought chases me as I rush toward home. Along with another thought:

How much does Mother know?

A case could be made for sleeping with Sam in order to get closer to the mayor. As a means of acquiring my target. I can explain that to Mother. I can make her understand.

Maybe I will tell Mother everything that's been going on. I will talk to her about my hesitations. I'll tell her about the Presence, and the men who speak Arabic. We will reason things out together, find the best way to finish the assignment.

The moment I walk through the door of my apartment, a Game Center notification pops up.

Mother has challenged me.

There is nothing more secure than a secure line. But there is a problem. The source and the destination are single points. No matter how much scrambling or how many servers the digital signals pass through in between, each one is still originating from a single point.

This is why communication with my superiors is always playacting.

But there is an alternate protocol. Kids all over the world use it every day.

MMORPG. Massively multiplayer online role-playing game.

Tens of thousands of voices at the same time. We can speak more freely there, but only in case of emergency.

A Game Center notification is Mother's version of the panic button, and she has pressed it.

I put away my iPhone.

I sit in front of the flat-screen television in the living room and power up the game box I find there.

Headset on. Controller at the ready.

I open *Zombie Crushed Dead!*, a first-person shooter.

Level six. Map four. "Hunter becomes the hunted."

Character selection: Marine Corporal.

Weapon selection: M4 Carbine Assault Rifle.

Begin.

Mother's voice.

"What the hell are you doing?" she says.

Angry.

I've never heard Mother lose her temper, and it's doubtful she's losing it now. It's more likely something of an opening gambit, meant to shock.

It does the trick. My breath turns ragged in my chest, and my palms begin to sweat around the controller.

In the game I am a zombie hunter. I walk through a town in flames, buildings empty of life, the undead stalking around me.

"Answer me," Mother says.

Voice only. No character.

The god voice.

"I did not finish my assignment," I say. As I speak, the mouth of my character moves. "I did not finish *yet*, I meant to say."

"You've been at the mayor's residence twice," Mother says.

"I haven't been alone with him," I say. "The scenario hasn't been right."

A pause.

"You're making excuses?" Mother says.

"Realities."

"Nothing has ever stopped you before."

"This time is different."

I turn a corner, empty a clip into a horde of zombies coming toward me. One of them screams in agony. "Why? Why?" it begs me.

"This is not a normal assignment," I say. "You said so yourself. You passed me a message to be careful, that there were new factors this time."

Other voices, other players surround me. Players from all over the world. They taunt one another. They boast. They bluff. They look for zombie sex.

"So you're saying it's my fault," Mother says. "I've given you more than you can handle?"

"Absolutely not," I say.

"Then what's stopping you from finishing your assignment?"

I don't answer.

"Your behavior is questionable," Mother says.

Questionable. The word sends a shiver through me.

A zombie moans, the sound echoing off the surrounding hillside.

"We knew this was going to happen sooner or later," Mother says.

"This?"

"A girlfriend."

"I don't have a girlfriend," I say.

A zombie horde runs at me. I dodge left, trip over a tree trunk. I'm nearly overcome by the mob.

I make it to my feet at the last second.

"We expected it," Mother says. "We even tried to prepare you for it. Do you remember?"

The first girl.

We slept together that night at her house. It was my first time away from The Program. I thought we'd fallen for each other. I thought I was normal, even if just for a night.

I didn't know that Mother had arranged the whole thing.

"I remember," I say.

"But it's happened now, on this assignment. You have good taste, but lousy timing."

"I don't have taste."

"You think you don't, but you do. I'm the one who trained you.
I know you better than you know yourself."

One of the zombies is not quite dead. Cut in half, but still
crawling toward me, its hunger unabated.

I put a bullet in its skull.

"I'd like to come home," I say.

I don't plan to say it. It pops out of me, almost like it's coming
from another boy. One I don't know very well.

"Home?" Mother says.

I hear the surprise in her voice.

"Just for a while," I say. "To see you."

It's been two years since I've seen the woman I'm speaking to. I
have no idea where she is. Back at the training house? In another
location? Even now as I look for her inside the zombie world, I
can't find her. I'm talking to myself, to the air, to the dead gray sky.

"You want to see us?" she says.

"Is it so strange to want to see my parents?"

"You've never asked before."

I look at the burning landscape around me.

Empty. All of it empty.

"Maybe things are different now," I say.

There's a long pause. A shutter slaps against the window of a
deserted house.

"I'm worried about you," Mother says. "You're getting confused. You might be in over your head. Perhaps we should take
you out of school."

I've pushed too far. This line of questioning, this unprofessional
request.

I'm exposed and in danger. I can sense it.

"No," I say, too quickly.

I slow my breathing, make my voice strong.

"I want to finish the assignment," I say. "Like I always do."

"I see," Mother says.

"You said it before—you know me. You know what I'm capable of."

A pause.

"The assignment has changed," Mother says. "Your target is being adjusted."

"Adjusted in what way?"

A target adjustment in midassignment. This has never happened before.

"The daughter. She is your new target."

"Sam?"

"Yes."

"What about the mayor?"

"Off the field."

A flash of anger hits behind my eyes. No more running. I switch weapons to the M40A5 sniper rifle.

"Can you handle that?" Mother says.

My mind is racing. I bite the inside of my lip until I taste blood. I use the pain to focus my thoughts down to a single laser point.

"I can handle anything," I say.

There. Up in the hills behind the abandoned hospital. A flash of something.

Glowing green eyes like a cat at night.

"Put aside your doubts," Mother says. "Whatever questions have been holding you up."

I switch to the sniper scope.

"You're out of time now," Mother says. "Pick up the phone and call the girl."

"Mother—" I say, and then I stop. I've already said too much.

Instead I look for her through the lens of the sniper scope.

"Finish, and then we can talk about you coming home for a visit," Mother says.

There's a clicking sound.

"I believe in you," she says, her voice fading away.

I swing the rifle around, bring it to bear where the eyes were.

They're gone.

I TRY REACHING SAM.

It goes to voice mail. Twice. Three times.

A test. That's what Father called this assignment.

I thought he meant it was a test of my skill level, but now I'm wondering if it's something else.

A test of my loyalty.

But that doesn't make sense. I have proven myself loyal in training and across six missions.

Unless—

Unless there are doubts about me.

Is that what Mother is doing—changing the assignment as a test of my allegiance?

I've never known her to act out of malice. The cruelest things she has done have only been to make me stronger. To teach me lessons I needed to learn.

Occam's razor. The simplest solution is the most probable.

The simplest solution: This is not about allegiance.

It's an assignment. Pure and simple.

Which would mean that Sam is guilty.

But that can't be true. What could Sam be guilty of that would make her the focus of The Program? The Program is about finding and removing enemies of the U.S. Not about girls with dead mothers, girls caught up in political turmoil because of decisions by their fathers.

The mayor. He was the original target.

If I can prove he's guilty, that would mean Sam is innocent. And my target would revert back to the mayor.

I dial Sam's number again, and for the fourth time the phone goes to voice mail. This time I leave a message: "We need to talk. Call as soon as you get this."

Eleven PM.

I pace the living room, struggling to get perspective on the chessboard of this assignment. How am I going to prove who is guilty when I don't know what they're guilty of?

Sam said she's helping her father with something tomorrow.

Tomorrow. The final day.

That's the key. Whatever's happening has caused my timeline to speed up.

How can I find out what it is?

It's eleven PM on a Friday night. I can't go back to the mayor's. Sam isn't answering my calls. And I can't talk to Father about this.

I'm stuck.

That's when I remember.

I'm not stuck. I have Howard.

That's what I tell Howard when I call him from the Korean grocery on the corner. I buy two throwaway phones and use one to make the call to Howard. I can't risk using my iPhone, because The Program is likely able to log the call.

If Mother knew I was breaking protocol to get help with the assignment—

We would all be in danger.

In any case, Howard is more than happy to hear from me.

Ten minutes later I'm standing in his bedroom. Computer cables snake across the floor. Lights twinkle and fans whir. His bedroom smells like sweat and electricity.

He wasn't kidding about being a hacker.

"What's going on?" he says.

"I have to tell you something, and I need you to listen and consider it carefully. Can you do that?"

His face turns serious.

"Of course."

I pause, thinking over what I'm about to do. I've been pushing the boundaries during this assignment, but I've never done anything like this.

A direct breach of protocol.

It is unprecedented. And there's no turning back.

I hesitate, wondering if there's some other way that I might have overlooked.

Then I think of Sam. And of my timeline.

"Today at school," I say, "you told me you thought I was different. You were right."

"I knew it," Howard says.

"I have a special job. Nobody in the world knows about it."

"What kind of job?"

How can I put this?

"I'm a soldier," I say.

"Like in the army?"

"No army. Just me."

"An army of one," he says. "I want to help."

I take a step toward him.

"If you help me, Howard, it will be very dangerous for you."

"Walking down the hall in school is dangerous for me."

He's got a point.

"But this is dangerous on another level," I say. "Whatever you do for me has to stay secret. Nobody can know. Not Sam, not Goji."

"It sounds exciting," he says, a big smile on his face.

I think about myself training with The Program early on. My first weapons class. My first martial arts class.

It seemed exciting.

Then it got real.

I say, "There are lives at stake."

"Whose life?"

"Sam's."

His smile fades. A siren wails as a police car goes by outside.

"What do you want me to do?" he says.

"I need to know the mayor's schedule tomorrow."

"I can do that."

The siren continues on, the sound fading into the night.

Howard grabs a keyboard and starts typing.

"How do you know what to look for?" I say.

"I've looked around City Hall stuff before," he says.

I stare at him.

"I had a little crush on Sam," he says. "But it was before I met Goji. I swear."

"I believe you."

He types some more.

"This isn't as straightforward as it should be," he says.

"What do you mean?"

"I checked public records, now I'm going internal—but there's a security blackout on the schedule."

"Why would that be?"

"I just have to crack—ah, this explains it," he says. "The Israeli prime minister is in town. He's in Washington talking about the new peace initiative—and then he's coming up here for a private meeting with the mayor. That's a little strange, isn't it?"

It would be, except he's not meeting the mayor. He's meeting the next special envoy. Or maybe he's trying to persuade the mayor to take the position.

But Howard doesn't need to know that.

"It looks like it was originally scheduled for Sunday," Howard says, "but it was moved up a day at the last minute."

Bingo.

"Why was it moved?"

"It's not clear. But the reception was moved, too," Howard says.

"Reception?"

"Invitation only. At Gracie Mansion tomorrow night."

My assignment was obviously shifted to reflect the change in schedule.

But why?

Why would The Program need to stop the mayor from meeting with the PM?

"Is that the information you needed?" Howard says.

I nod. "Good job," I say.

Howard looks proud.

"That wasn't so bad," he says.

"I may need you for other, more difficult things."

"Deal," he says.

I take out the second throwaway phone.

"We'll use these if we need to communicate."

I head for the door, but then I stop.

"One more thing," I say.

I type the mayor's name into a search engine and follow the links until I arrive at the archived news article about his wife's death. I find the photo I saw in the library, the one from the funeral for Sam's mother.

"I remember that photo," Howard says with a sigh.

"Look behind Sam," I say.

I point to the soldier, the one whose eyes are looking toward Sam while everyone else looks straight ahead. The same soldier I saw in the picture in her bedroom.

"I want to know who the soldier is. Can you find out?"

"You don't need a hacker for that," Howard says.

"What do you mean?"

"I know who it is. That's Sam's boyfriend, Gideon. He was a soldier in the Israeli Defense Forces."

I DO NOT SLEEP.

I lie in bed for hours, trying to work the angles on the assignment. Every one leads to a dead end.

I've been trained to get close to my mark and gain access. But I'm not an investigator. This is a different skill set.

Then again, maybe not. Maybe there's a way to apply my skills to the problem.

Instead of trying to solve the equation, I relax and give my intuition a chance to work.

I do what I do in a normal assignment. I project my attention through the data set, and I open myself to cracks in the story, things that seem out of place.

The mayor's blog.

Something about it doesn't feel right.

It's nearly two AM, but I get out of bed and call Howard. He answers on the first ring.

"You're awake," I say.

"Are you kidding? I can't sleep after—after the things you told me."

Howard's hesitation is a good thing. He knows not to say too much on the phone, even on a throwaway phone.

"The mayor has a new blog," I say.

"Sam told me about it when it launched. Not so interesting."

"I saw him taking pictures for it the other night. Can you bring it up on your computer?"

I hear keys clicking, and a second later Howard says, "I'm looking at a birthday cake."

"Anything seem strange about it?"

"Pink frosting. You'd expect the mayor to have something a little more masculine."

"The frosting was white," I say. "I was there."

"There's some distortion in the color range. Might be my monitor."

There's a pause as he adjusts something.

"It's still off," he says.

"Take a closer look, would you? Something feels wrong about the blog."

"I'll check it out," he says.

"Call me if you find anything," I say.

I get back into bed and watch the clock pass three, then four. Each hour brings me closer to my final day.

And with it, my new assignment.

Sam.

It doesn't seem like I fall asleep, but it must happen eventually because I'm awakened by banging at my door.

At first I think it's a dream, but when I open my eyes, there is sunlight pouring through the blinds.

And the banging continues.

I immediately roll out of bed and hit the floor, prepared to defend myself. My body does it reflexively. Rapid change of position, deflect focus, gain initiative.

The knocking again. Urgent.

Only one person knows where I live. One person and The Program.

And The Program doesn't knock.

I move toward the door, expecting to find Sam.

"Ben!" a voice shouts.

Darius.

I open the door. Darius is standing there, breathing heavily.

"How did you get up here?"

"Your neighbor let me in. Sam's in trouble. She needs to see you right away."

"She sent you?"

"How the hell else would I know where you lived?"

"Why didn't she call me?"

"I don't know. She said I'm the only one she could trust and she sent me to get you."

"Where is she now?" I say.

"Around the corner. The playground at Riverside Park."

I look at Darius, at his facial expression, at the way he holds his body, clutching his fingers until they turn white.

He's worried.

I grab my iPhone and the throwaway, toss the rest of my tools in a backpack. I slide my ballpoint pen into my jacket pocket.

"Let's go," I say.

I glance at the apartment one final time. My location has been revealed, the apartment burned. I'll have to send a weather advisory to have it sanitized.

The things I shared with Sam here. They are just memories now.

I close the door, hear the lock click in place.

When we get outside the building, Darius turns away from the park.

"I'm not coming with you," Darius says.

"Why not?"

"Sam said not to."

He starts to go, then turns back. He touches my arm.

"Take care of her, Ben."

He means it.

CHILDREN SCREAM.

They run through the playground, laughing, and fighting, and falling over one another.

Saturday morning. The final day.

I walk around the playground, scanning for Sam. Parents look up briefly as I walk by, scouting for members of their tribe. When they see I do not belong, they dismiss me.

Sam arrives in a hurry a minute later. She's wearing running tights and a baseball cap pulled low over her eyes. Her ponytail is stuck through the hole in the back. A simple look that is an instant disguise. Two clothing items and she appears no different from forty percent of the women in New York.

Sam looks around cautiously. She spots me and comes over.

"What's going on?" I say.

Her eyes dart around the park. She starts to walk, beckons me to follow. She circles the playground and stops at a spot off the main path behind some bushes.

"Why did you send Darius to my place?"

"I didn't know what else to do," Sam says. "I couldn't go myself."

There's something on the edge of my awareness. Hovering just outside my range of perception.

"Remember I told you about my ex?" she says.

"I remember."

I feel it now. The Presence.

"He's back," Sam says.

I think of the picture of Sam with the Israeli soldier.

Gideon. That's what Howard said his name was.

"Your ex is in New York?"

"He's been here for a while. I didn't tell you about it."

"Why not?"

"Because I was trying to figure out how to handle things."

"What is there to handle?"

"Don't yell at me, Ben."

"I'm not yelling."

But my voice is too loud. I speak quickly, the words clipped. I listen to myself as I do it. I try to focus on what Sam is saying and track the Presence at the same time, but I cannot. Instead of listening to Sam, I project my energy into the park, trying to locate the Presence. He's here somewhere, moving through the trees that border the park.

Sam is still talking. The words are coming out of her, but they have no meaning.

I focus back on her.

"There's too much history between us," she says. "I owe him a lot, and I'm confused."

"You weren't confused last night."

I bite the inside of my mouth. The soft part, a little below the lip.

"Last night was perfect," she says.

"So perfect that you're going back to your ex?"

"You're not understanding me, Ben. He knows about you."

"How does he know?"

"I told him. This was before—before I had feelings for you."

"So he knows about me. What's the big deal?"

"He's not a normal person."

I laugh. I lick the inside of my lip. The familiar taste of blood hits my tongue.

"I'm not afraid of your jealous boyfriend," I say.

"He's not jealous," she says.

"What is he?"

"There's a bigger picture. Something you can't see."

"Help me to see it."

She looks around the park.

"I can't," she says.

"You mean you won't."

"Don't make this hard on me."

I've heard these words before. Not from a person. I have to think about where I have heard them.

In a movie.

Yes. These are things girls say in movies.

Things they say when they break up.

Sam looks at me, but something is different. She does not look at me the way she did last night.

I try to focus on my assignment.

The questions I had. The reasons for the questions.

All far away.

I reach to my pocket. I feel the hard outline of the pen through the leather.

You have a new target. That's what Mother told me.

My target is standing in front of me.

A sensation comes over me. Pressure behind my eyes and in my throat.

This sensation. What is it?

IT CAME WHEN I WAS TWELVE.

The sensation.

Mike led me into the special house for the first time, up a long staircase with wooden steps that did not creak and a railing that did not sway. I walked across a floor that had no give in it.

Real houses are alive with sound. They shift with the wind and creak when you walk. They bend to the people who live in them.

Not this house.

It looked like a house inside and out, but it was something else. Something dead.

Mike led me to a door, but he did not open it for me.

I had to do that on my own. The first of many choices I would be asked to make in the coming days.

The door swung open without a sound.

It was a home office. Dark wood, books, silver picture frames on a shelf. A big window looked out on a distant bank of trees. Sunlight streamed in, falling in patches across a large mahogany desk.

Behind the desk sat a woman.

Mother.

"Welcome," she said.

And she smiled.

I was twelve years old. My father was dead. My mother was gone.

I was in a strange place, a strange house, with a strange woman smiling at me.

I knew I was trapped and in danger, but my mind would not believe it. So I smiled at the woman smiling at me. At the woman I would come to know as Mother.

I remember that day. That moment. The smile.

I felt it then.

This sensation.

Not a sensation, I realize now.

A feeling.

FEAR.

I feel it as Sam looks through me in the park.

"Please stay away from me," she says. "You're in danger."

She reaches out and touches my arm.

"I don't want anything bad to happen to you. I mean that."

She turns and walks away.

My heart races even though I am not moving.

I am in Riverside Park. Children run through the playground, change direction, then run the opposite way. They clump and separate like a flock of birds.

The birds scream.

Am I in danger?

The mothers do not react to the screams. Their expressions remain unchanged, tired eyes and fake smiles.

The children scream.

I am walking. When did I start walking?

The ground feels strange beneath my feet. Wind cool on my forehead.

Why cool?

I am sweating. That is why the wind feels cool.

Be careful.

Footsteps behind me.

The Presence.

I turn to face him.

But it's not the Presence. The energy is coming from another direction.

I turn again.

It's Sam, I think. *She's come back to talk. She's changed her mind, and we're going to find a way to make this work.*

But I don't see Sam, either.

"Zach," a voice says.

It's a voice I know well.

My best friend is calling me. He is calling me with a name I have not heard spoken in years. A name I put away a long time ago.

My name.

"Zach," the voice says again.

It's Mike.

I turn toward him.

It is a mistake.

A LIGHT SHINES IN MY EYES.

I awaken from unconsciousness bound to a chair, my arms on its arms, my legs on its legs. A lover's embrace, sealed in duct tape.

How long have I been out? There's no way to know, no windows for me to judge time of day.

I try to move my head to look around, but that, too, has been immobilized.

A figure appears in front of me, coming into focus in the bright lights.

I was right.

It's Mike.

He is older. His hair is different and the angles in his face are deeper. But there's no question that it's him.

"Are you with me, buddy?" he says.

He snaps his fingers until my eyes focus.

"Zach-arach. Wake up."

That voice. For a moment it feels as though we're sitting in a burger place after school in Rochester. I'm back in my first life, and no time has passed at all.

But this is not the past. It's now. I'm watching Mike walk back and forth, eyeing me.

"You let the daughter go," he says.

I cannot say anything. My mouth is gagged.

"I want to think you have a plan," Mike says, "that you couldn't finish in the park just now, because you have a better plan. Am I right?"

This seems absurd, this asking of questions to a person who cannot answer. It is an interrogation technique designed to drive the mind to frenzy. You cannot speak, cannot protest or defend yourself. The questions bounce around in your head until your defenses break down and you tell the truth just to make it stop.

I've been trained in the same technique. I can defend myself against it.

Mike says, "Truth be known, I don't believe you have a plan. I think you're down the rabbit hole."

I stare at him.

"Do you love her, Zach? Is that what's going on?"

I don't move, don't blink. I give him nothing.

He shakes his head. "There's no such thing. I thought we taught you that."

I test the tape on my wrists. Heavy-duty duct tape. You can't fight your way out of that kind of tape.

"Whatever's driving you, you've pissed off a lot of people. Not me, of course. I don't get angry. But she does."

Mother.

"*I can barely sleep at night.* That's what she said when we talked about you. I'll be honest—I'm not sure that woman ever sleeps."

Mike laughs. Then he stretches, pacing back and forth in a short pattern.

A pattern.

I file this in my memory. Mike moves in a pattern when he's thinking. It's unconscious. It's a weakness.

I might need this information later.

If there is a later.

"They sent me here," he says. "I argued against it, against it being me, but they said I was the one. We have history, they said. They thought that would be important."

He nods like he knows what they meant.

"FYI, I went to bat for you. Not that it makes any difference now. But I think you should know. Certain parties lobbied for pulling you out altogether."

He separates the words when he says them. *Pulling. You. Out.*

Does Mother pull people out of jobs?

How many of us are there? How many more like me?

"I argued against it, Zach. I said they should allow you to finish the job. We all stumble. It even happened to me once."

He takes a deep breath.

"Once."

He reaches into his pocket, removes an eyeglass case. He takes out a tiny screwdriver, the kind used to adjust the screws on eye-glass frames. He turns the end of the screwdriver.

I have not seen this particular variation. But I know what it is.

An injection device.

"This argument went on for a good, long while, Zach. It got

heated. There were even questions about your loyalty. Your family history was mentioned. Not by me, of course."

A brief swell of something inside me. I think of Mother in a room surrounded by faceless people, discussing my behavior. Is this what happened to my father? Was there a meeting to discuss his behavior? A decision was made.

And then Mike came.

"Mother listened to all sides," Mike said. "And then she decided you would be allowed to complete the assignment, albeit with certain fail-safes in place."

He steps toward me, the plunger held close to his body. This is good on his part. If for some reason I got free, I couldn't knock it out of his hands.

"Fail-safe. That's me. You fail, I make sure The Program stays safe."

He examines the tape on my feet and arms. Examines them from a distance.

"And you failed. The great Zach Abram failed. There's no other way to say it."

I shiver at hearing my name. It makes me think of my father's name. Joseph Abram.

Professor Abram.

Mike circles around behind me.

This is how it will end. Silently and from behind.

"Have you thought about this moment?" he says.

The end.

I didn't know there would be an end. Not for me.

I've thought of another moment. The moment of meeting Mike again. This was not how I imagined it would go.

"I've thought about it myself," Mike says. "What it would feel like to be in that chair. I didn't know if it would suck, or—"

He exhales slowly.

"Or maybe it would be a relief. To be done with it all."

He rubs his face.

"You probably haven't thought about things like that yet. This is still exciting to you, isn't it? Running around and playing soldier. But then, I'm a little older than you."

How old is Mike now? Early twenties maybe. It's hard to tell. His face looks different from different angles. One minute he looks like a boy, the next like an old man.

"Ah, shit," he says. "I'm sorry to have to do it."

He takes a breath, just like I've been trained to do.

There is a moment of not knowing, followed by the pressure of Mike's knuckles against the soft skin of my neck.

It is intimate, his warm fingers in that sensitive place. I know that they hold the plunger. When he depresses it, I will be gone in a few breaths.

I will not beg. I will not cry. I will not give him the satisfaction of shouting out to him or to a God I barely know. I will not reach for the places terrified people reach to.

I inhale and exhale, slowing my breathing.

My last thought.

Will it be hatred for Mike? For Mother?

No. I will choose something else.

A memory of my parents. My birth parents.

I see them now. Not on the last day, or even those last months when things turned dark in our house.

I remember a time before that.

My father is smiling; his arms are around my mother. They are standing in the kitchen of our house in Rochester and laughing.

I walk into the room. They notice me, and their arms extend, welcoming me into the circle.

An embrace of three.

This will be my last thought.

Mike says, "Mother doesn't know what happened in the park just now."

He whispers in my ear.

"She doesn't know, because I haven't told her."

The knuckles of one hand stay against my neck, while his other hand touches my own. He puts something cold and flat on my thumb, then he closes my index finger so whatever it is gets pinched in place there.

His hand moves away from my neck.

"I figure I owe you one, Zach."

He comes back around so he's standing in front of me. We look at each other.

"Finish the assignment and everything goes back to the way it was."

I don't move, don't so much as blink. I give him nothing at all.

"If you don't do it for The Program," he says, "then do it for your father."

What does he mean? My father is dead.

This is a lie. A trick.

I follow Mike with my eyes. I watch him for signs of the tell, but I don't see any.

He steps out of my peripheral vision, just a voice now.

"You remind me a lot of him. Certain aspects."

His footsteps recede into the darkness.

"He's alive, Zach. Your father. Do you understand what I'm saying?"

I hear a door open somewhere out of view.

"Finish," he says.

And then he's gone.

I pinch my fingers to feel what he put down there. It's a piece of metal the size of a postage stamp. It is nearly dull, but there is the tiniest bit of edge on it.

Just enough edge to cut through tape.

IT'S DARK WHEN I HIT THE STREET.

A warehouse district, someplace I don't recognize. Empty loading docks and bricks covered with graffiti. MESEROLE STREET, the sign says.

My father.

He's all I can think about.

I follow the sound of beeping horns until I hit a main thoroughfare. Bushwick Avenue. I'm in Brooklyn. I follow the road north to Grand Street, and I get on an L train headed into the city.

I find an empty seat and let my thoughts drift as the train car rocks.

My father.

I see him taped to a chair in the living room, his head bowed, chin nearly on his chest. His shirt was covered in blood. I feel Mike's arm around me like it was that day. I was drugged, barely able to stand on my own. He led me into the room and showed me to my father.

My father was still alive then.

And after?

I never saw him again.

My father has been dead for years. That is what I've believed.

But I did not see him die.

I saw him in that chair, I saw him taped and hurting and covered in blood, but I did not see what happened after.

I was told that he was dead. That's different from having evidence.

But he must be dead.

Time is proof. How long has it been? Nearly five years now. If my father were alive, he would have come for me.

Unless he doesn't know I'm alive.

Mike has given me a second chance. A final chance.

If I'm going to find out what happened to my father, I have to complete this assignment.

The train crosses into Manhattan and pulls into the station.

Eight PM. My final night. I have to get to Gracie Mansion.

But first I have to check with Howard. I race to the surface so I can get a signal.

The screen of the throwaway lights up with texts from Howard. Eight of them, all the same.

Call me 911, they say.

"I'VE TRIED YOU A THOUSAND TIMES," HOWARD SAYS.

"I ran into some trouble," I say.

"I didn't know what to do. I didn't know if something had happened—"

Mike was right. I'm down the rabbit hole. I broke protocol out of desperation, and now I've got someone working for me with no emergency procedures in place and no contingencies. I am exposed. So is Howard.

It's time to end it.

"Forget about all of this, Howard. Shut it down."

"But you were right about the mayor's blog," he says.

"How was I right?"

"The photos on the blog were tampered with. It's so subtle that I missed it at first. The photos look strange because someone has changed the color value of each red pixel in the JPEG to match a byte of an rtf document."

"You're saying there are documents hidden inside the pictures on the blog?"

"Not just any documents. High-level stuff. Homeland Security memos sent to the mayor's office. Surveillance reports of suspected terror cells in the New York area."

I set out to get proof of the mayor's guilt. Now I have it.

But if the mayor is guilty, why did Mother change my target to Sam?

"Why does the mayor have secret documents on his blog?" Howard says.

"Because he's transmitting them to someone. Can you tell who is receiving them?"

"That's the genius of it," Howard says. "There's no way to know. The data is public, but it's broken down into a million pixels. You can't read it unless you're on the other end with a filter program that pieces it back together."

I run the facts through my head again.

The mayor is revealing Homeland Security secrets to someone. Maybe it doesn't matter why. I'm trying to save Sam, and now I have proof that her father is guilty.

"I have to get to Gracie Mansion," I say to Howard.

"Wait, Ben. There's something else you need to know. The last post. It contains the plans for the meeting tonight. All the security protocols. Everything."

"That means someone knows the mayor is meeting with the Israeli prime minister."

"But who?" Howard says.

I TAKE THE EXPRESS TRAIN TO 86TH STREET.

I get out of the station, and I run.

I turn onto East End Avenue, and I'm immediately stopped by flashing lights. There's a two-block NYPD security cordon around Gracie, a sea of blue uniforms liberally sprinkled with dark suits.

Concentric circles. That's what I'm imagining in my mind.

NYPD doing the grunt work around the edges. Israeli security and agents from the Diplomatic Service in the center.

Guests are already entering, ferried down a single access path. This is no high school party. There's no walking up to the door and talking your way in, and I don't have Erica to use as an excuse.

In almost every circumstance, I could slip into an event undetected. But not here, not where professionals are on duty, actively looking for anything unusual in the environment.

They are looking for the unusual, so I must be something familiar.

I'm wearing a button-down shirt over a T-shirt. I untuck the button-down, let it hang loosely around me. I take my wallet out and slip it into my waistband under the shirt. Now I have the telltale bulge of a weapon worn by an undercover cop.

I head south a few blocks and enter Carl Schurz Park at a corner, appearing among the police officers there. I match my energy to theirs. I am an undercover working the south side of the park, one of several scattered through the area.

I pass through a group of officers. A sergeant nods to me.

The nod.

I nod back and keep going.

The park has been cordoned off, but I only need to puncture the outer layer of the cordon and get to the inside. It's the inherent weakness of the cordon strategy. If you are outside, you are presumed dangerous. But once you're inside, it's assumed that you've been granted access by those on the outer edges.

So I aim toward the center, and I keep going.

By the time I make it through the second cordon, my shirt is neatly tucked in, my wallet is in my pocket where it belongs, and I am moving like a teenager who's out of his league. I look in awe at the dignitaries entering Gracie. I lick my fingers and use them to try to make my hair look neat.

I'm close enough now to hear the clink of glasses and people's voices inside the mansion.

I am almost inside.

Almost.

"Stop," the voice says.

Behind me. The Pro from the mayor's apartment.

He's outside the mansion doing a recon lap when he stumbles on me.

Bad luck on my part. Good training on his.

"Phew. Somebody I recognize." I say it like I'm happy to see him.

"Your invitation," he says. "I need it."

"They took it at the front gate."

"No, they didn't. You have to show it at every entry point."

I glance toward the front door of Gracie. Sure enough, they're checking invitations one final time.

"You caught me," I say.

I notice his earpiece and attached microphone. A tap at his collar, and security will swarm us. But he doesn't tap. Not yet.

"I caught you what?" he says.

"Maybe I should have said you caught Sam. Sneaking me in."

He nods, listening.

"How often do you get to shake hands with a prime minister, right?" I say. "She told me to meet her outside and she'd bring me in."

I'm quite sure the PM's visit is secret. That's why I mention him. How would I know he was here unless I'd been invited by Sam?

I see him considering.

"If she's meeting you, where is she?" he says.

"That's what I'm wondering right now."

"Me, too," he says.

He reaches toward his collar—

"When Sam comes, I hope she brings toilet paper with her," I say.

"Toilet paper?" he says.

"Because I'm shitting my pants right now."

He laughs. He puts his hand down without calling for backup.

"You're a funny guy," he says. "Come on. I'll take you inside."

I follow him into Gracie Mansion.

WE PASS THROUGH A GRAND FOYER CROWDED WITH DIGNITARIES.

Some I recognize from the news, some I do not. Politicians, businessmen, diplomats.

Members of the Jewish community and representatives from the Arab League. Some foreign accents, Israeli and Arabic both. Some may disagree with this prime minister's approach, but it's hard to fault his passion on the issue of peace.

The Pro leads me into the blue-walled Wagner Wing ballroom. It's not a huge crowd—maybe fifty people standing in clumps, waiting.

"Do you see Sam?" I say.

He stands next to me scanning the room. She's not here.

Something comes over his earpiece. He holds his hand to his ear, listening.

He scowls.

"Behave yourself," he says to me. "I've got work."

And he leaves me alone.

The energy in the room changes, excitement rippling through the crowd. Suddenly the prime minister enters through a side door with the mayor at his side. The room bursts into applause.

The prime minister grins, greeting people and shaking hands as he works the crowd.

The mayor is a more familiar face and not nearly as exciting to the room. People pass by him with firm handshakes and smiles on their way to the prime minister.

I scan the space, looking for Sam, but I don't see her.

I move toward the mayor.

I'm running variables in my head.

First is the idea that Mother is wrong. The mayor is the guilty party. His blog is more or less proof of this.

Maybe if I complete my original assignment, I can prove it to her.

Security is reduced around the mayor. He is not a visiting dignitary, so he's not watched as closely. I can do it here, in front of the entire crowd. Do it silently. Do it in a handshake, then fade away as the circles constrict around him.

Ten steps from the mayor.

Sam comes into the room. I notice her from the corner of my eye, passing through a side hallway into the ballroom.

We see each other at the same time.

Her eyes widen in surprise—

And then she turns and rushes out of the room.

"I didn't know Sam invited you," the mayor says.

He's seen me from across the room and come over.

"She got me on the list," I say. "I was just coming over to say congratulations."

He hesitates. How would I know what's going on unless Sam had really invited me?

"It's not congratulations yet," he says. "I'm still mayor until the end of the year."

"And then special envoy?"

"We're talking about it, Ben. Still talk at this point."

"Forgive me, but that seems very different from the work you've been doing."

"Ah, but it's a thrilling time in Israel. The prime minister is determined to find a lasting peace with his neighbors. He feels it's time, and our government couldn't agree more. The world has changed; the Arab Spring has created new possibilities for everyone. We have a rare opportunity to make a difference together. That's a mission I'd like to be a part of."

But if that's the case, why would the mayor leak security plans for this event? Leak them to whom?

"Sir, the things we discussed at dinner the other night. I was hoping to talk to you further—"

"About Sam."

"I'm worried about her. I understand if now is not a good time."

"Nonsense. This is important. Let's step away for a moment, Ben."

THE MAYOR TAKES ME INTO A SMALL RECEPTION ROOM.

I scan the corners for security cameras. I see two of them. No way of knowing what kind of lens is in the cameras. A fish-eye that scans the entire room but distorts it, or wide angles that photograph a slice.

If it's the latter, I can move the mayor into a blind zone along the wall. There will be evidence that I was with him in the room, but no evidence of what happened here.

Not if I do this right. I take the pen from my pocket and slide it up the sleeve by my wrist.

"Can I offer you something?" the mayor says.

He's moving to the blind zone himself, a liquor cabinet along the side wall.

"A bourbon. Neat," I say.

He laughs.

"How about a Diet Coke instead?"

"That works, too."

I walk over and join him at the cabinet.

"Tell me about Sam," he says.

"I talked to her this morning," I say. "She's a mess."

He sighs. He pulls the cigarette case from his breast pocket, glances around to make sure we're alone. Then he cracks the window and lights up.

"She doesn't want to go back to Israel, does she?" he says.

"Your wife's accident. It's got a lot of bad memories for her."

"The accident. Yes."

I read the tension in his forehead.

"It wasn't an accident, was it?"

"Sam told you," he says.

Sam didn't tell me anything, but I nod.

"She told me as much as she was comfortable with," I say.

"I fear we made a mistake keeping it a secret, but you understand, it was a decision at the highest level. Post–9/11. Two wars in progress at the time. The Middle East was a powder keg. Add the wife of a popular American politician being killed in a bombing attack. Who knows what might have happened."

A terror attack. That's how Sam's mother really died.

"We suffered quietly," the mayor says. "We mourned quietly. It seemed like the right choice at the time. But I'm afraid it was too much to ask of Sam. She changed after that."

You changed, too, I think.

The mayor is working for someone now, passing secrets through his blog. Maybe he's motivated by vengeance. Maybe other reasons.

The motivation doesn't matter. Only the facts do.

All the questions, all the risks, and I'm back to where I started.

The mayor. My original assignment.

My time is up.

I've decided. I will kill the mayor, and I will deal with the consequences after.

I will deal with Mother.

I let the pen slide into my hand. I turn the cap to weaponize it.

A text chimes on my phone.

I glance at it.

It's Howard with another 911.

I hesitate.

"Do you need a moment?" the mayor says.

I stare at the 911 message.

"I'm sorry, sir."

"Do what you need to do, and then I want to talk about how we can help Sam."

I walk to the other side of the room, through the path of the cameras. Twice now through the path.

I keep eyes on the mayor as I dial Howard. He answers, his voice high and tense.

"Another photo just went up on the mayor's blog," Howard says.

"That's impossible," I say.

"Thirty seconds ago."

I cover my mouth and whisper into the phone.

"I'm with the mayor. He couldn't have posted anything."

"It's not a document this time. There's a picture embedded in the photo."

"A picture of what, Howard?"

"Of you. On the street at night."

The picture Sam took of me.

I turn to the mayor.

"Who posts to your blog?" I say.

"That's a strange question," he says.

"It's important, sir."

"I write the posts. But Sam's in charge of the blog. She takes care of everything for me."

The leaked documents on the blog. They're not coming from the mayor.

They're coming from Sam.

I turn my back and press the phone to my lips. "Close everything down, Howard. Cover your tracks."

I shut off the phone, return the pen to safe mode.

"We have to find Sam," I say to the mayor. "It's an emergency."

Suddenly an explosion rumbles through the mansion, shaking the floor under our feet. The power goes out, accompanied by shouts from the ballroom.

The doors burst open, and the mayor's security detail rushes in with guns drawn.

"Freeze!" It's the Pro from the mayor's apartment. He's looking straight at me.

The other security people run at the mayor, surrounding him.

"What's happening?" the mayor says.

"There's an emergency. We have to go. Now," one of them says.

They start to hustle the mayor out of the room. The Pro's got a Glock trained on my chest. The big one, forty-five cal. Thirteen rounds in the magazine, one in the chamber.

I may not use guns, but I respect them. Especially when they're pointed at me.

I don't move.

"Get the mayor out of here," the Pro says to the security team.

He keeps the gun on me.

The mayor stops in midstride. He's nearly knocked over by his own security men.

"That's Ben!" he shouts over the urgings of his security men. "He's with me."

The Pro blinks twice, deciding what to do.

I project surprise. I project fear.

Anything that might keep him from pulling the trigger.

The Pro makes his choice. He lowers his pistol.

Then he rushes toward me, grabs me by the arm, and groups me with the mayor, bringing me inside the safety of the security cordon.

"Let's move!" the Pro shouts, and his team hustles us out of the room.

THE SCENT OF EXPLOSIVES FILLS THE HALLWAY.

The emergency lights flicker red as we move in a group through the smoke-filled halls of Gracie. There is confusion all around us, various security teams struggling to bring order to chaos as they evacuate the guests.

"Where is my daughter?" the mayor says.

"Working on finding her, sir," the Pro says. "In the meantime we're taking you and the prime minister to the safe room."

He shouts at the security detail, and they lead us deeper into the mansion, down a passageway to a secure staircase. The Pro types in a code, the door opens, and he guides us down the stairs and into a basement hallway.

I'm moving with the security team, letting them carry me along, but I'm thinking about the mayor's blog and the emergency-response protocols that were revealed there. Somebody knows every move we're making. Not just us. The prime minister as well.

Two key players. But which one is the target?

Loud voices speaking Hebrew in front of us.

We turn the corner and two Israeli agents are shouting into radios. They are down at the end of the hall, barely distinguishable in the red haze.

"Friendlies!" the Pro shouts. "We have the mayor with us."

The Israelis wave to us, signaling that the hallway is clear.

The mayor and I are shepherded forward, surrounded by the security team.

"Where is the prime minister?" an Israeli asks the Pro.

"I haven't seen him," the Pro says.

"Be careful," the Israeli says. "We don't know what's happening here."

The men nod to one another, and the Pro urges our group forward.

We head down the hall until we approach another corner. There's a subtle shift in the lighting, a momentary shadow caused by someone passing in front of a distant light source.

The security people don't see it, but I do.

They rush forward, and I pretend to stumble. There's a domino effect as our group slows down around me. The Pro quickly scoops me up and gets me back on my feet.

It doesn't take more than a second. Just enough to slow our forward momentum so we don't run around the corner.

Into what's waiting.

Two men with ski masks wearing new nylon jackets like the Gap guys on the subway.

But the ski masks have pistols.

They turn toward us. The mayor is in front of me, blocking the shot. The masked men take aim, but they don't fire.

They don't want to hit the mayor.

I shift to the left, and their weapons follow me.

Our security guys do not hesitate. They open fire, instantly mowing the two men down.

The Pro glances at me. He senses something is off, but he's not sure what it is.

I can see he wants to ask me, but how is he going to interrogate a frightened kid in the middle of a firefight?

"Keep moving!" he says to the group.

"Stay close, Ben," the mayor says.

Suddenly a secondary explosion rocks the building. The sound is distant and muffled, originating somewhere below us.

The explosions are coming from the basement. That's where I need to be.

The hall goes black as the explosion knocks out the red emergency lighting. The Pro leads our group forward, the pace slowed to a crawl because of the smoke and darkness.

I use the confusion to slip away from the mayor. He's in good hands with the Pro, and he'll be safer without me around.

I double back down the hallway to the bodies of the masked men sprawled on the ground.

I check the first one. He's dead.

The second one groans. He's all but gone, bleeding from half a dozen critical wounds.

I roll him over, pull up his mask.

He coughs blood, his eyes distant. His lips are moving.

I lean down and put my ear near his face.

He's praying. In Hebrew.

These are Israelis—that's what I think now. But they are not the Israeli security team with the prime minister. They are a different team, men who are working with the Presence.

I'm starting to put this together. It's the Presence who has been reading the blog, the Presence who needed the security plans to Gracie. It's he and his men who have been following me.

I have a good idea who he is. And where I might find him.

I follow the thickening smoke toward the basement.

EMPTY DUFFEL BAGS ARE STREWN AROUND A UTILITY ROOM IN THE BASEMENT.

I've found the staging area for the attack, but there are no people here. I check surrounding doors, looking for the point of entry into Gracie, but I don't find anything.

It could mean I missed it, or it could mean they were let in by someone with access.

Someone like Sam.

The Presence is close now. I can sense him. I use the darkness and smoke to make my way through the basement hallway. I creep forward until I hear voices up ahead, arguing.

I peek into the room. A custodial office and changing area.

Men in shiny nylon jackets, all of them in masks, all of them speaking Hebrew.

The Presence is here.

He's standing across the room wearing a mask, but I recognize his posture immediately.

He shouts at the other men, and they nod the way soldiers do when they're taking orders.

Suddenly the men race out of the room. I slam my body back against the wall. They turn as they come out, running away from me without looking back.

Only the Presence is left inside.

I step into the room.

The Presence freezes. He stands still, watching me. The fabric around his mouth moves. Is it a smile?

"Your friends are gone," I say.

"And you are alone," he says in heavily accented English.

There's a gun in his waistband. He reaches for it.

I'm too far away to jump him, and I don't have a weapon of my own.

My best bet is to wait for the shot. If I move at the moment he pulls the trigger, it will reduce his effectiveness. How much will depend on how well trained he is.

He lifts his pistol, extending it toward me—

"Gideon," I say.

He hesitates for a moment.

"You know me?" he says.

"I've seen your photo," I say. "In Sam's bedroom."

The muscles in his jaw tense through the mask.

"And I've seen yours," he says. "Sam sent it to me. So I could kill you."

He pulls off his mask.

I see his face up close for the first time. Curly hair, dark eyes, and a beard.

I saw him in the Apple Store the first day, again in the subway the other night.

The Presence.

Now I understand why he looked familiar to me.

The Presence is Gideon.

He's older now and he has a beard. That's why I couldn't immediately connect him to the soldier in the photos with Sam. Only his eyes are the same, cold and dead, the eyes of a soldier.

"You are the famous Ben," he says.

He puts the pistol down on the table next to him.

"This will be for my men who you killed," he says.

"Not for Sam?"

"Sam can take care of herself," he says.

And he leaps at me.

He is shockingly fast, crossing the room in two large hops and attacking with vicious, well-aimed punches to my chest and head.

I knock the first few away, take the last in the chest. Hard.

He backs up, snorting, excited by the fight.

"I saw you in the Apple Store," I say. "You've been after me from the very beginning."

"I've been after you since Sam called me."

"How did she know?"

"A strange man appears in her class days before a mission. That wouldn't set off alarm bells for you?"

"It would. But I'm trained to see things like that."

"So is Sam. By me."

He shouts and comes fast with a series of kicks. Again, he's on top of me before I can adjust. I manage to knock the first kick away with my forearm, but the second catches me on the side and sends me flying into the wall.

He fights emotionally, each attack a highly focused wave of anger and violence.

I'm not familiar with this style. Training and emotion tend to cancel each other out. I've fought disciplined men, their moves calculated and deadly. I've fought emotional ones who rush in and try to overwhelm.

I know how to handle both kinds.

But this is something else.

I need to keep him talking, distract him long enough to get my bearings.

"You recruited Sam in Israel after her mother's death," I say.

"It was not so difficult. A girl whose mother was killed in a bombing attack. A girl as emotional as Sam. And so very useful because of her father."

Without warning he comes again. He rushes directly toward me, jinking away at the last second, running halfway up the wall and using it to propel him sideways in a flying kick that sends me crashing through a table.

"She thinks you love her," I say.

"I do love her," he says.

I turn just in time to see him swinging a table leg down at my head like a club.

Boom. He misses by an inch.

"You used her," I say.

Boom. I jerk at the last second and he misses again.

"And what did you do to her?" he says.

Boom. A third time.

I've had enough. I torque backward, spring off my hands, and kick him in the chest with both legs. He goes flying into a metal locker.

"So you do know how to fight," he says.

We rush each other, meeting in the center of the room. I attack high and low at the same time, testing for weaknesses in his defense. No matter how well trained, most people will favor one side or another, one zone more than the next. If I can find his weak point—

A hand closes around my neck.

Gideon. He's somehow reached through my attack and grasped me by the throat.

"You're thinking when you should be fighting," he says. "That is a problem."

"I don't need a lesson from you."

I clench the muscles in my neck, fighting the pincer grip.

"A final lesson," he says.

The grip tightens, cutting off the blood flow to my brain.

I have seconds before losing consciousness—

"Gideon!" Sam shouts.

His grip loosens for a millisecond, and I thrash out at him, an open palm to the chin followed by an elbow that connects to his nose with an ugly crunch. He goes sprawling across the room, nearly crashing into Sam.

Sam.

In the doorway now. Watching.

"Samara, get out of here," Gideon says.

He says her name with a Hebrew pronunciation.

"What are you going to do, Gideon?" she says.

He steps toward me, but Sam stops him with a hand on his chest.

"Tell me," she says.

His body softens. I see the intimacy in the gesture between them.

I say, "Does she know that you're going to kill her father?"

"What?" Sam says.

"Don't listen to him," Gideon says. "Your father is not our objective."

The prime minister. He's the target.

Sam didn't know this, which means she didn't know about tonight. Not the details, at least. But she knew what she was doing when she put the plans on the blog.

And when she gave them my photo.

"I thought you were Israeli," I say.

"Proudly," he says.

"Why are you attacking your own man?"

"I'm following instructions," he says. "Just as I believe you are."

"Whose instructions?"

"A group within a group within a group. You know how these things work." He looks at Sam. "You told me he was smart," Gideon says.

Sam stares at the ground.

"But your men are wearing masks and speaking Arabic," I say.

"That's the brilliance of it. Somewhere in Queens, the police are kicking down a doorway right now, finding evidence of a homegrown terror cell. They are the ones who are responsible for tonight."

"That's why you're playing Halloween down here. You want it to look like terrorism."

"You have to admit it's a nice twist," he says.

He turns to Sam. He puts a hand on her cheek.

"You do not need to be here now," he says. "This man is not your friend. He was sent to hurt you."

She looks at me.

"Is that true, Ben?"

Is it true?

Yes. But I deviated from the plan.

I can't explain that to her now, so I say nothing at all.

"You see?" Gideon says.

He steps away so that Sam and I are facing each other across the room.

"I didn't want it to come to this," Sam says. "I tried to warn you to stay away."

"You can still stop it," I say.

"I can't."

"I don't think you knew about the plot tonight."

I reach for her, but she doesn't move.

"I may not have known, but I knew other things. I'm in too deep, Ben. There's no turning back."

"Why did you do it?" I say.

"For my mother. For the country she loved."

She gives me a sad half smile.

And then she goes out the door.

A flash of movement to my left.

Gideon is darting out of the room through an opening to a utility tunnel hidden in the darkness behind him.

I'm guessing that he's heading for the safe room. The prime minister will be there by now, along with the mayor.

I look to the hallway door, toward Sam.

I lied to her. My assignment is not to stop this.

My assignment is to stop her.

But for some reason, I'm thinking about the mayor, about our time together, the way he put his trust in me and invited me into his life.

I should not care about this. Or about him. He is neither the target of my assignment nor my responsibility.

But he is in danger. And the prime minister with him.

If my primary assignment was meant to prevent the attack at Gracie tonight, is it possible I should intercede now?

Without instructions from The Program, I have no way to know.

No way but to follow my intuition.

Sam in the hallway. Gideon in the opposite direction through the utility tunnel, heading for the mayor and the prime minister.

Me in the middle of it all.

I make a choice.

I follow Gideon into the tunnel.

THE SOUND IS NEARLY IMPERCEPTIBLE.

A single strand of fishing line stretched almost to breaking, followed by the click of a mechanical switch.

Nearly imperceptible, but not entirely. Because when my foot hits the trip wire at the entrance to the utility tunnel, I hear it.

Too late to undo what I've done, but quick enough to throw myself forward and down, jamming my body between the floor and the wall as an explosion turns the air to fire behind me. Fragments of shrapnel ping off the concrete wall inches above my head.

I avoid the deadliest effects of the blast, but not all of it. The pressure wave slaps me against the ground, stunning me. The roar turns to silence as my ears stop working.

My father. His image appears in my head. Not the image of him in his office when he was alive, or the final time I saw him tied to the chair. A different image, one I've never actually seen.

My father alive in a room somewhere, standing at a window, thinking about me. Wondering if I'm alive or dead.

The smell of smoke brings me back.

I am on the ground in the blackness of the utility tunnel. I check my limbs, and they are functional. I check my flesh for wounds, but there are none.

I look back to a small stream of light coming from the entrance to the custodian's office. The tunnel is still open. I can escape.

But I don't.

I crawl deeper into the darkness.

Gideon is somewhere up ahead. I must stop him.

After a few yards, the smoke begins to clear, and I can see a string of LED lights lining the floor. The light is dim, just enough to navigate.

I stay low, crawling beneath the layer of smoke. My guess is that there is one more booby trap at the exit. Entrance and exit. That's how I'd rig the tunnel if it were me. I'm betting that's what Gideon has done, too.

I accelerate, moving through the darkness faster and faster, turning corners quickly, projecting my attention forward toward Gideon.

Four rapid turns and I sense him.

Then I see him.

Around the next corner. The light of the exit behind him, his shadow moving in front of me. Moving quickly. Moving carelessly.

He's not watching his back, probably because he thinks the explosion took me down. All his focus is on finishing the mission in front of him. I've had the same blinders on, so I know what it feels like. I also know it's a mistake.

Especially right now.

I rush forward and grab him from behind, my arm hooking

around his neck. He's startled, but he adjusts quickly. It's a narrow tunnel, so he keeps driving his way forward, kicking at me and trying to get me to release.

I don't let go, so he adjusts his strategy, twisting around quickly and catching me with a head butt that sends me flying backward.

"You will not give up," Gideon says.

"No."

"Well, then. I found something I like about you."

He pulls an object from a hidden sheath beneath his jacket.

It's a knife.

The blade is dark carbon steel, designed for fighting in darkness without giving away its position. It swishes through the air, the sound the only indication of its deadly trajectory.

I remember a knife like this. It was in Mike's hands. I remember the shock as it pierced my shoulder, and the pain that followed as my nerves registered the assault.

I made a mistake that day long ago with Mike. I fought the knife instead of fighting Mike. And I lost.

I will not make the same mistake again.

Gideon attacks with a lunge, and I take a double step backward in the narrow tunnel. The blade passes in front of me without making contact.

Gideon moves toward me, and I allow it. There is a turn in the tunnel a few steps behind me. I want to keep him talking, keep him moving forward.

"The prime minister is a great man," I say. "What will killing him gain you?"

"Great men make mistakes, too. His particular mistakes are not for me to know. I have orders. I follow them. It's easier that way."

He's right about that. It's easier when you don't think, don't challenge what you've been told. Maybe you don't end up in tunnels fighting for your life. Or maybe you do. But it's not because you made the decision—it's because that's what you've been sent to do.

Soldiers like Gideon and me are trained not to make decisions on our own.

So why am I here?

I'm here to save the mayor's life.

Gideon steps forward, slashing as he comes; I leap back and around the corner, and he follows. He's entirely focused on me as the target. He doesn't realize there's a wall behind him now.

"I think your mission has failed," I say.

"You're thinking again," he says. "I guess you didn't learn your lesson."

I shout and rush at him like an emotional fighter enraged. I open my arms like I'm going to trap him in a bear hug.

He is surprised by my gambit, but pleased, too. I know because I can feel him relax the slightest bit. He's goaded me into making a mistake and fighting outside my style. I'm fighting like him—that's what he believes.

There's even a hint of a smile on his lips.

It's easy to fight a maniac. You just stay out of range of his anger and then you take him down.

This is what he tries.

He drops back to avoid my wild parry, not realizing he's fallen out of position and the turn in the tunnel is behind him. He bumps into the wall.

There's a moment of shock as he discovers he's trapped.

A moment. That's all it takes to convert my mad rush into

something else. Something much more deliberate. Instead of grabbing for a bear hug, I strike out with a leg, so quickly he doesn't see it coming.

A single kick folds him at the waist. He clutches his stomach as the knife clatters to the floor.

I grab him then, and I use the inertia to turn the corner and throw him as hard as I can toward the exit of the tunnel.

He falls backward, his body spinning out of control, tumbling until his upper body crosses past the exit of the tunnel and into the light on the other side.

He sits up quickly, and he smiles back at me.

He's thinking that I blew it, and he's won.

He didn't hear the click of the fishing line triggering the explosives at the exit, where he'd wired them.

But I did.

Gideon is emotional, but he is predictable, too. This is a mistake for people in our business.

I fling myself around the corner to safety, and a second later an explosion rocks the tunnel, tearing him apart and sealing the exit forever.

I RACE AFTER SAM.

I double back through the tunnel to the custodian closet, then through the hallway to an outer door that's propped open.

I pop out onto a hidden corner of the estate. Bent blades of grass leading away from the mansion.

I think as Sam would think, move as she would move.

Where would she go now? Would she stay in Carl Schurz Park?

She could walk up to any law enforcement official, say she's the mayor's daughter, and ask for help. She would be safe then, outside the zone of suspicion.

But I think there is a different plan.

A plan with Gideon. A meeting place for after. It has to be someplace safe, someplace she feels comfortable and where she will not be recognized. Someplace that gives them access to different avenues of escape.

Someplace like Cleopatra's Needle.

SHE STANDS IN SHADOW BEHIND THE STATUE.

I step into the plaza, into the moonlight.

"Ben?"

"Who did you expect?"

She doesn't answer. She watches me, her expression unchanged.

"I know about the blog," I say. "The secrets you were passing to Gideon and his people. All of it."

"I owe him my life," Sam says. "He was there for me after my mother died."

"He recruited you."

"In hindsight, yes. At the time it didn't seem like that."

"What did it seem like?"

"Love."

I think of Mike, the way he came into my life like a brother.

I say, "He pretended he loved you so he could turn you. That's not love."

"I guess you'd know all about that," she says.

We're on opposite sides of the statue, subtly shifting back and forth as we speak. My step countered by her step, hers by my own.

"You were playing me from the beginning," I say. "You had Gideon following me the day we met."

"To watch you, not to hurt you. It wasn't until you killed his man in the brownstone that we knew for sure you weren't who you said you were."

"You knew, but you moved forward with our relationship anyway?"

"I knew something, but I didn't know what you were here for. Not exactly. I needed to keep you close until I could find out."

"So that's that. It was all a game for you."

"No," she says. "It was real for me."

She comes around the statue until we're facing each other across the plaza.

"What was it for you?" she says.

"An assignment."

"That's all?"

I want to tell her everything. How it began as an assignment, how I hesitated and it became something else.

I want to tell her, but I don't.

I say, "I needed to be close to you so I could get to your father."

"He was your target?"

"Originally, yes."

"And now?"

I look at her face in the moonlight. She is more beautiful than when I first saw her, but she is something else, too. Something darker. Something like me.

"You committed espionage," I say. "You put your father and the entire country at risk."

"Is that why you're here, Ben? You're some kind of spy hunter?"

"I'm a soldier."

"And I suppose right and wrong don't matter?"

I shrug. "I do what I'm told," I say.

I'm supposed to. I didn't complete this assignment because of her. But I don't tell her that.

"Oh, I remember," she says. "You're the boy who doesn't believe in anything. We're different that way. I not only believe, I'm willing to back it up with action."

"That's how you justify treason?"

"The Israelis are U.S. allies. If you share secrets with a friend, that's not treason."

"Is that what Gideon told you?"

"Gideon," she says.

She looks around the empty plaza.

"He won't be coming," I say.

Her face changes. Her eyes turn cold.

The same look I saw from Gideon, from Mike. The same thing I see in the mirror when I look at myself.

"You're not who I hoped you would be," she says.

"Neither are you."

I step toward her.

I'm expecting her to run. I'm ready for it, another chase through the park. Like the first time, but with a much different intent.

But she doesn't run. She starts to cry.

Maybe she's crying for Gideon, maybe for herself. I want to think it's for me, but I don't know.

I've seen women cry before—women *and* men—and it doesn't move me.

This is different.

When I see Sam crying, I want to comfort her. I want to put my arms around her one last time, even if just for a moment. I reach for her—

And she turns on me, snarling.

Not the Sam I know, the girl I met in AP European class at school. Someone else.

A beast, furious and dangerous.

She comes at me with a barrage of kicks and punches. I recognize elements of jujitsu and Krav Maga. I recognize them only briefly, because then there is contact, and we are in the fight.

It's obvious that Sam was trained at some point, but also obvious that it was a long time ago. She's got more potential than skill. She tries to make up for it with rage.

Rage can be effective in short bursts, even deadly. But not over multiple attacks, and not against a well-matched opponent.

Not against me.

When she comes at me with a roar followed by a series of vicious kicks, it looks impressive, but she is exerting too much energy.

It's a primary lesson of combat. By fighting too hard, she is fighting herself. And when you fight yourself, you always lose.

I stay in close and make myself an available target. A final flurry of punches, and her performance degrades quickly. She's tired.

That's when I strike.

I use my body as a fulcrum, and I take her down, flat on her back.

She tries to get up, and I take her down again.

I think of Gideon with his hand on her cheek, the way they looked at each other in the basement.

She comes up a third time, and I slam her down hard. She is panting and exhausted, her energy spent.

I stand over her.

I stay out of arm's reach. I don't take unnecessary risks with her, not anymore.

"You don't have to do this, Ben," she says.

She uses my name. I know this trick. Personalize the conflict, create a bond with your attacker, then plead for mercy.

It sounds heartfelt, but it does not move me.

"My name is not Ben," I say.

She looks up at me.

"Whoever you are," she says, "you don't have to do it."

"I have no choice," I say.

"There's always a choice," she says.

She made a choice. To betray her father and betray her country. But there is no choice for me. Not really.

I slip the pen from my pocket. She looks at it, her eyes wide.

"It doesn't hurt," I say.

"How do you know?" she says.

I turn the pen cap to the right, click it once, and feel the soft *pop* between my fingers as the fluid is released into the point. An idea comes to mind. A new thought, irritating, like an itch in a place you can't reach.

I'll push the point into myself instead of Sam.

Nothing dramatic. I'll press it into the soft skin at my wrist.

It will be quick. Even with my conditioning, I will have, what? Seven seconds instead of three? An extra breath or two. No more.

I should press the point into myself. That's what I'm thinking. Then I will know how it feels, I will know whether or not it hurts, and Sam will walk away.

The idea gives me peace. Until I think of Mike.

Because this will not stand. Mother will not let it stand.

Perhaps Mike is still here, and they will let him out of his cage. Mother will tell him to make a lesson of it.

Sam will lie to him at first, say that we fought, say she got the upper hand.

But eventually the truth will come out.

She'll tell him how in the last moment I flip-flopped and pressed the pen point into myself. She'll say that I chose myself over her because we were in a relationship.

In the back of his mind, he'll know she's telling the truth, but he won't let it end like that. Mother won't allow it to end like that.

That's what I realize as I'm standing over Sam. Pressing the point into myself won't change anything.

Correction: It will change everything for me. But for Sam, nothing at all. For her, it will likely make things worse.

I adjust the angle of the pen, the point now exposed and facing its true target.

"Where are you?" Sam says.

"Far away," I say.

She reaches for my ankle, and I pull it back.

She looks up at me, startled. Maybe she wasn't trying to hurt me. Maybe she wants to connect with me. Even in this last moment.

I cannot allow it.

"Please tell me your name," she says.

"Why?"

"I want to know who you really are."

"I'm nobody," I say.

And I lean over and press the point of the pen into the side of her neck.

It takes three seconds, no more. Her eyes flutter and close.

And it's done.

I lean over to make sure. My wrists brush the sides of her breasts. They are soft. Too soft.

"Does it hurt?" I say.

I say it to myself. I'm the only one left.

And then her lips part. I think I'm imagining it, but when I look closer, her lips are moving. She's trying to speak. I lean down toward her.

"You were right," she whispers. "It doesn't hurt."

I step back, surprised.

Did I click the pen once or twice?

I made a mistake. This is what I think. I've injected the coma drug by mistake. Sam will keep breathing, and the choice I have made will be undone.

There will be another choice, a better choice, a choice I didn't have the courage to make.

We will run away. Start over in a new place. We will make a home together in a distant city where nobody knows who we are, and where we will never be found.

A sensation passes through my chest.

Not a sensation. Something else. A feeling.

Love.

"Samara," I say.

She doesn't answer.

I press an ear to her lips, check the pulse point in her neck.

Nothing.

I didn't make a mistake with the pen. I don't make mistakes.

Sam is like everyone else I've met.

Dead.

A twig snaps across the plaza. A police officer is standing at the edge of the clearing, watching me.

Not a police officer. Mike, dressed in a police uniform.

"Welcome back," he says.

"Back?"

"Back home. To the family."

His face is obscured by darkness.

"You made the right choice," Mike says.

Did I?

I look down at Sam's body at my feet.

"You'll let Mother know I finished the assignment," I say.

"She already knows."

But was it enough? I didn't prevent the attack at Gracie or the threat on the prime minister's life.

I watch Mike's center mass. That's how you know which way a person is going to move. Not their arms or hands or legs—those can trick you. But his stomach. That moves in only one direction—the direction he's going to go.

If he comes toward me, then I will know it wasn't enough.

We will fight for the second time in our lives.

I will not let him get the upper hand this time. I will subdue him and ask him some questions.

I want to know about my father.

And then I want to punish him.

Him and The Program. Mother. I want to take them all down.

For my father, for Sam.

For stealing my life from me.

I watch his center mass, but it does not approach. It recedes, withdrawing deeper into shadow.

It was enough. For now.

"Maybe we'll see each other again," Mike says.

"I hope so," I say.

"It's not up to us."

"It's never up to us."

"Good luck, Zach," he says, and he disappears.

I could follow him. Track him like an animal in the park. Settle this thing between us.

I don't.

Not today.

Not the news of an attack at Gracie Mansion. Instead there is a story about a gas line explosion on the Upper East Side. Neighbors heard two large booms, and Gracie Mansion had to be evacuated in the middle of an event.

That's at the bottom of the front page, but it's the lead article that matters most. The story of the untimely death of the mayor's daughter. Of natural causes.

There will be an inquiry. That's what the papers say. Teens are not supposed to die for no reason at all, but it happens. A football player collapses. An otherwise healthy girl keels over from a rare defect in a blood vessel.

Accidents, illness, genetics, bad luck.

There are a thousand ways to die.

The mayor appears at a news conference, his face twisted by grief.

I watch it on television in the New York hotel room where I am temporarily staying. I stand close to the screen and turn down the sound. I follow the mayor's eyes as he speaks, looking for any signs of falsehood.

There are none.

Sam was right. Her father is a great actor.

Not when it comes to his grief. That seems genuine.

But he has no problem lying about the rest of the story. What he was doing with the prime minister, and what happened afterward. The powers that be have decided to keep the real story of the Gracie Mansion attack a secret.

Whatever element hatched the assassination plot against the PM has failed. The peace process will move forward, perhaps with the mayor attached after his term ends.

My phone vibrates in its cradle, the double vibrations of the Poker app.

I turn off the television, and I take Mother's call.

"We've made arrangements at school," she says.

The cover story: My father has been transferred for work, so I must transfer. Another rich kid drifting into school and out, caught up in the vagaries of influential parents' lives.

Nothing unusual about that. Not at our school.

Their school, I should say.

Not mine.

"You'll put in an appearance on Monday," Mother says. "Give you a chance to say your good-byes."

Normally I'm gone immediately after an assignment, but because of the high-profile nature of this assignment and my exposure during it, it's been decided that I should linger briefly. Let attention fade for a day or two.

"You did a lot of work this time out," Mother says. "A lot of unassigned work."

"Proof," I say.

"What is that?"

"That's what I was working on in trigonometry."

"Proof. Is that part of the syllabus?" Mother says.

"Not exactly."

"You've never deviated from the syllabus before," she says. "Was it really necessary?"

I should be extremely careful with Mother now. I should back down, play timid, be apologetic.

I think of Sam's lifeless body at my feet in the park.

Suddenly I am angry at Mother, at the assignments she doles out so casually and from a distance. I'm angry at myself for always doing what I'm told. Too angry for business as usual.

"This time it was necessary," I say.

"Couldn't you have finished the assignment without proof?" she says.

No anger in her voice. Only curiosity.

"If I had finished at the beginning, I would have turned in the wrong solution," I say. "Even you have to acknowledge that. You changed the assignment in midcourse."

"True," she says. "But think it through. Puzzle it out."

Puzzle It Out.

One of the games we played in the house when I was training.

Mother would raise a question that seemed to have an obvious solution. As soon as I had the answer, I'd shout it out, thinking I was brilliant.

Then Mother would take me deeper. Show me paths I couldn't see on my own.

Puzzle It Out.

"The original assignment," Mother says. "Didn't you have the solution at the very beginning?"

The mayor. He was my original target, and I was in his office on day one.

I say, "If I'd finished the assignment that first day, I would have been making a mistake."

Because the mayor was not guilty of anything more than loving his daughter, perhaps giving her too much leeway. I would have killed an innocent person.

The Program made the mistake, not me.

It was my investigation that revealed the guilty party.

Unless—

I take a moment to puzzle it out.

If I had removed the mayor, there would have been no need for the PM to visit.

No meeting at Gracie.

Nothing for Gideon to accomplish.

And Sam?

With her father dead, she would have been neutralized, her access to information gone. There would have been no target adjustment. Sam would still be alive, and the mayor would be dead.

And the problem, such as it was, would be gone.

If I'd acted on that first day, it would have been over. Quickly and easily.

So I took the wrong path.

"It's because you waited that new information was revealed," Mother says. "That's why we had to adjust the assignment. If you had acted, there would have been no need."

Like she's in my head. Like she's always been there, ten steps ahead of me, plotting.

"Your old mom is not so stupid," she says. "Maybe you'll trust her the next time she tells you what to do."

Ten steps ahead, but not all-seeing. Because how did I get the proof?

She hasn't asked me about it. Which means she doesn't know about Howard.

Not yet.

She may or may not know that Mike gave me a second chance.

And what Mike told me about my father?

"You said that after I was finished we could talk about my coming home."

"I did say that."

"I'd like to see you and Dad."

"We'd like to see you, too. But with the move going on, it's not the right time."

"You're moving?" I say.

"In a manner of speaking."

"Could you make some time for me?"

"I'm sorry, honey. Our hands are tied," she says.

Tied.

I think of myself taped to a chair in a dark warehouse, Mike looming over me.

Sent by Mother.

I think of my father taped to a chair in our living room, a trickle of blood running down his face. Mike stands over him.

Sent by Mother.

"There's a lot more we need to talk about," I say.

"Oh, yes," Mother says. "We will."

I hear her typing on a keyboard in the background. Is she writing a report about what happened here? Putting everything in neat boxes?

Maybe this was just another assignment to her, another task checked off the list. An operative deviated slightly from the plan, but he's back now.

Zach Abram is back in the family.

Mission accomplished.

She says, "By the way, keep your eye out for an e-mail. Your father is sending you something."

"I'll look forward to it," I say. "I have to go now, Mom. There's a lot to do before I leave."

"Love you," she says.

I start to speak, but I cannot. My throat is dry.

I take a breath. I swallow. And I stick to the script.

"Love you. Talk to you soon," I say.

I end the call.

"I KNEW YOU'D COME," HOWARD SAYS.

I stand in his bedroom doorway.

The apartment is empty, his parents gone. That will only make my job easier.

On the desk monitors behind him, windows are open to dozens of different news sources. Sam's death and the aftermath from every angle and perspective.

"Were you there when Sam…"

His voice trails off.

"I didn't see her," I lie. "But I know she didn't suffer."

That part is the truth.

Howard starts to cry. "Did I have anything to do with it?"

"You tried to prevent it. We both did."

"Is that what we were doing?"

"Yes."

That seems to calm him.

"She was always nice to me," he says.

"She wasn't who she seemed to be," I say.

"Are any of us?"

The monitors behind him go to screen saver. Goji's avatar floats in a starry sky, her eyes massive and glowing bright. Her face travels on a journey from one monitor to the next.

Howard says, "Some columnist at the *Daily News* said the mayor should run for president in the next election. Can you believe it? They're already using this for politics."

"I imagine there will be a lot of that in the days to come."

Howard sniffles, wiping his nose with his sleeve. After a minute, he pulls himself together.

"I want to show you something," he says. "I did some more work for you."

He flicks the mouse, and one of his screens turns on. Long lists of numbers that I can't understand.

"What am I looking at?"

"When I was working for you, I kept running across trails. Everywhere I went—the blog, the mayor's schedule—someone had already been there."

"The Israelis were involved. Was it them?"

"I don't think so. These were hackers. This one kid in particular. Infinite is his name."

"Infinite?"

"That's his handle. Infinite L∞P. With an infinity sign instead of letters, like that means something."

"How do you know about him?"

"He's a twelve-year-old dickwad, that's how. He thinks he's a genius, and I can't totally disagree with him, given the things he can do. But he's arrogant, so he doesn't clean up after himself.

There's a vapor trail that I followed to Spotify. He listens to Katy Perry. Does that sound like a genius to you?"

"You're saying there's a little kid who's a hacker?"

"Not just one. A whole bunch of them, all in different cities. I thought you'd know about them. Because of your job."

"I don't know."

But maybe The Program does. I imagine kids implanted all over the country, doing the tech work for The Program while I do the wet work.

"So you've been looking around online," I say.

"I was trying to help you," he says.

There are seven steps between us. I use two of them.

"I covered my tracks," Howard says, fear creeping into his voice.

"You did your best. I'm not saying you didn't."

I take another step.

"I know I'm a loose end," he says.

A loose end. He's right. That's why I've come. To clean up loose ends.

I take another step toward him. He lowers his head and stares at the ground.

"Kill me if you want," he says. "You'd be doing me a favor."

"I don't want to kill you," I say.

The problem is Mother.

My rebellion was tolerated, at least for the time being. But she knows only part of it. It's one thing to breach protocol myself, but if she knew I'd potentially revealed The Program to an outsider—

I don't want to kill Howard, but I can't leave any evidence.

Howard is evidence. Even though we've maintained anonymity to this point, there's no telling what will happen going forward.

Howard might not be able to keep his mouth shut. He'll brag to someone at school. He'll tell Goji. And he can link me back to the mayor and Sam.

Kill only when necessary. This is my training.

I've thought it through and decided that Howard is a risk I cannot take.

It will look like suicide.

Howard was obsessed with Sam. Everyone in school knew it. He's mentally unstable, with medical records that prove as much.

People will say that Sam's death sent Howard over the edge. The biggest loser in school lost his secret crush, and the grief was too much for him.

The pieces of the story are already in place. I need only to write the ending.

"Could I send a good-bye e-mail to Goji?" Howard says. "At least you can give me that before you do it."

"Stop saying that, Howard."

I look at him squeezed into the corner of his room. It seems he's always in a corner. Corner of his room, corner of the cafeteria, corner of the hall.

In a corner being hit. The story of Howard's life.

No matter now.

I can't take him with me, and I can't leave him here knowing what he knows.

But what if I could use him in some way? What if his skills could still be helpful to me?

There's always a choice. That's what Sam said.

Which means I can choose differently.

"You found the hackers," I say.

"Yes."

"Could you find out who they work for?"

"Very possible," Howard says.

Could you find The Program?

That's the real question.

I sit on the edge of Howard's bed. It's the only part not covered in dirty clothes.

"What's happening?" Howard says.

Choices.

"I'm not going to hurt you," I say.

"You mean you're going to take me with you?"

"I can't do that. But I have another idea for how we can work together."

"Like what?" he says, getting excited.

"Go back to school, go back to your life, but it's not your life anymore. It's your cover story. Because you're working for me now."

"Like a spy," he says.

"That's right. And if you have problems in school—"

"They're not really problems. They're part of my cover story."

"You got it," I say.

"This is incredible, Ben."

"We'll put a system in place. Encoded communications. You may not hear from me for long periods of time."

"I understand."

"Then I'll call on you. For your expertise."

"Anytime."

"Howard, you have to cover your tracks."

"Triple and quadruple cover," he says.

"Not like—what's his name?"

"Infinite L∞P. No. I'm better than him."

"It's not about better or worse. It's about what happens if you get found out. What happens to both of us."

He nods. "I understand the risks."

"Okay, then," I say. "You've got yourself a job."

He rushes over to the bed and throws his arms around me tightly.

"We won't be doing that," I say.

"Just one hug," he says. "Then it's all professional from here on out."

He finishes the hug, then steps back, a smile on his face.

"Thank you, Ben. Thanks for giving me a chance."

He watches Goji's face float on his computer monitor. He reaches out and touches the screen.

"Thanks for both of us," he says.

I glance at the screen. "She can't know anything," I say.

"Never," he says.

I step toward the door.

"What will you do now?" he says.

I look at my watch.

"Time for school," I say. "It's my last day."

CLASSES HAVE BEEN CANCELED, BUT SCHOOL IS OPEN.

There are counselors in the gym to assist us. There are clergy in the cafeteria to pray with us. There are teachers everywhere to support us.

Not us.

Them.

Students wander the halls, clumping in small groups. Those who knew Sam are falling apart. Those who didn't know her pretend to be.

I pass by Sam's locker. The floor is strewn with flowers, candles, and photos. Cards are tucked into bouquets, propped up on the floor, taped onto the locker itself.

Darius stands against the wall keeping silent vigil.

I clear my throat. He notices me standing there.

"I tried to protect her," he says. "You know I did."

I nod.

He says, "You want to know the part that really gets me? I never told her how I felt about her."

He kicks at an empty locker, his face a mask of pain.

"She knew," I say.

He looks up. "How can you be sure?"

"She told me."

His face relaxes, and he smiles just a little.

A girl with black hair walks up and collapses into his arms. I recognize her as one of Sam's posse that first day.

"What happened?" he asks her.

"What happened?" she says back to him.

It's the echo of the day. *What happened?* Followed by *I can't believe it.*

My e-mail chimes, and I check my phone.

Father sent me something. I follow the links as I've been taught to do.

It's not my next assignment. It's instructions. How to leave, which train to take. And a hotel in another city, where I will wait.

I look back at Darius. He is distracted talking to the girl, so I keep walking, letting my presence fade by degrees.

Sadness helps. It is distracting.

I help, pulling my energy back little by little until I am nearly gone from this place.

"I see you," Erica says.

Nearly.

"What do you see?" I say.

"Suffering."

I give her a half smile, like it might be true.

It's not true. I am not suffering.

I do not suffer.

"You loved her," Erica says.

"I hardly knew her," I say.

"You were falling in love. That's what I should have said. You were in the process."

I shake my head.

"I think you were. Maybe you didn't know it."

I feel a tug deep in my stomach.

I get still for a moment, explore the sensation.

Not a sensation.

A feeling.

I remember this feeling from a long time ago. It is like sadness, only worse. Much worse.

It's grief.

A deep chasm of grief. I'm standing on the edge looking into endless depths.

I cannot stay in this place. It's unbearable.

I step back from the edge.

I take the feeling and file it away along with the other things from this assignment. The things I've seen and the people I've met. Images flash through my mind.

Standing arm in arm with the mayor, singing together while Sam looks on with a cake in her hands.

Sam in my apartment in front of the fire.

Sam in the park. At my feet, unmoving.

Sam and the mayor, and all the memories that accompany them.

I do not need these things, only the lesson they have taught me.

What is the lesson?

"Are you okay, Ben?"

What is the lesson?

Survive.

No matter what happens to you, no matter the circumstances, no matter what life tosses at you—the losses, the pain.

You must survive.

"I'm fine," I tell Erica.

She looks at me. I make my face neutral.

"How are you doing, Erica?"

"I'm not fine. I want a drink so badly I can't stand it."

"You shouldn't drink when you're feeling like this."

"Thanks for the public service announcement," she says.

She puts a hand on my forearm.

"Sorry. I'm being a bitch. I know you care. It's just that I kind of hate you. You turned me down three times. Nobody does that and lives."

"Yet here I am, alive and well."

"I let you live," she says. "For Sam's sake. Maybe I'm getting cheesy in my old age."

"How old are you?"

"Nearly eighteen."

"That is old."

"Shut up," she says.

She punches me in the arm.

A challenge.

No.

Something else.

People are acting strangely today. Crying one minute, laughing the next. Flirting and hugging and falling apart.

Grief. This is what it does to people. It makes them strangers to themselves.

It's good that I've put it away.

"What am I going to do without her?" Erica says.

She groans and hugs herself.

This is not part of my training, grieving people and aftermath. I do not stay for aftermath. Not usually.

When in doubt, emulate.

"What are any of us going to do?" I say to Erica.

This seems to comfort her.

"Call me if you need anything," she says.

"I will."

"Promise me?"

I don't promise. I drift away.

I have instructions from Father now, and it's time to go.

I continue through the halls, my energy receding.

I move past clusters of grieving students, past teachers trying to comfort them, past empty classrooms and full halls. This is not my school anymore. I am no longer one of them.

Maybe I never was.

Eventually people stop looking at me, stop meeting my eye.

There is nothing to meet.

There is nobody here.

ACKNOWLEDGMENTS

Boy Nobody may be a solo act, but I most certainly am not.

I'd like to thank Rich Tackenberg, tech blogger and friend, whose analysis of technology and social media trends was enormously helpful to me in the preparation of this book.

Thanks to Kate Sullivan, my incredible editor, who found *I Am the Weapon*, championed it, and gave the series a home.

Special thanks to publisher Megan Tingley, who invited me into the LBYR family. And what a family it is—Andrew Smith, Melanie Chang, Eileen Lawrence, Victoria Stapleton, and Amy Habayeb, to name only a few. I look forward to making the journey with all of you.

Thanks to Sally Willcox at CAA for her tireless efforts to bring The Unknown Assassin to the big screen.

Finally I'd like to thank my agent, Stuart Krichevsky, and the SK team—Shana Cohen and Ross Harris. Stuart has guided me, grown with me, and believed in me over several years, several projects, and several bumps in the road. That's my idea of a great agent.

I STAND ON THE ROCKS HIGH ABOVE A LAKE.

The water below me is inky green, waves lapping gently against the banks of a shade-dappled cove. It's a warm summer's evening, but I know the water will be cool here under these trees.

Cool and deep.

We're not supposed to be here at all, much less climb the rocks and high-dive from the top. The camp counselors think it's dangerous, and they're right. If you angle it wrong, hit the shallow water, slip and tumble and smack the rocks, you could hurt yourself.

Or worse. You could break your neck. That's why this place is strictly off-limits.

Not that I care.

It is the evening of the third day since I've come here—a summer sports camp for boys located in southern Vermont near the New Hampshire border. I am a CIT, a counselor in training. Or so they think. There are campers and counselors who have met me, but they do not know who I am. My real identity.

They do not know there is a soldier among them.

I look at the water below me.

It's dangerous to jump from up here. That's what they say. Most kids are afraid to do it.

Not me.

I jump.

There's a thrilling sensation as I leap into space, open air around me, and then I am falling, falling, my speed increasing as I plunge headfirst into the lake. My angle is perfect and it sends me down through the water like a bullet. I kick to increase the depth of my dive, and the black bottom rushes up fast. For a second it looks like I misjudged, kicked too hard, and I'm going to smash into the lake floor and snap my neck. I stretch my arms out in front of me, brace for the sickening crunch of bone against rock.

It doesn't come.

The water resistance slows me down just in time for my fingertips to lightly touch the bottom.

I settle there. I pick up two heavy stones and hold them in my hands, using them to weigh me down.

I stay where it is quiet and dark, where no people or thoughts can disturb me. My last mission was only a week ago, but it seems far away now.

The girl seems far away. I can't see her face in the darkness.

I'm grateful for this.

My lungs are burning, the oxygen depleted in my system. I let them burn. The pain feels good.

I am trained to deal with pain, to absorb its intensity, spreading it across my body until it disperses through the entire neural network.

Physical pain is easy. It's the other kind that's new to me. The emotional kind.

My body is screaming for oxygen now, but I deny it, staying down an additional two minutes.

Pain control. It's good practice.

When I'm ready, I push off the bottom and hard-kick my way to the surface. That's when I see him. A boy standing on the riverbank, watching me.

How did I miss him? Even underwater, I should be able to detect this level of attention directed toward me.

The boy says, "You were down there so long I thought you were dead."

"You wish."

He smiles and so do I.

This boy's name is Peter. He is a CIT in the bunk next to mine. I met him three days ago, and he has become my friend. An instant and easy friend.

I am expert at making friends. It's what I've been taught to do.

Or at least pretend to do.

"I saw you jump from the cliff," Peter says, astonishment on his face.

"That's not a cliff," I say.

I climb out of the lake, shake water from my hair.

"It looks like a cliff to me," he says, looking up at the rocks. "A scary friggin' cliff."

"Everything is scary to you. You play soccer with a mouth guard."

"I like my teeth. You can't fault me for that."

"I like my teeth, too. But I'm not afraid to lose a couple for the cause."

"What cause? This isn't the army; it's a stupid sports camp."

The bell from the dining hall rings in the distance.

"Is it dinnertime already?" I say.

"Second bell. That's why I came to find you."

Two bells. We only get three. Then we miss dinner for being late.

They're trying to force some discipline onto the campers, and as CITs, we're supposed to lead by example.

"Let's get going," I say. "I'm starved."

I pick up my T-shirt from the bank where I left it earlier. I slip it on as we head to camp.

Peter turns his back to me, exposing himself to danger without knowing it. An attack from the blind spot is always the most effective. Before Peter realized what was happening, it would be too late.

"What are they serving tonight?" I say.

Peter looks back at me. I keep an appropriate distance, four feet. Nothing that will cause him to be alarmed.

"It's Fish Thursday," he says. "That means excessive stink factor."

I grin at him.

"You never laugh," he says.

"I laugh."

"You smile. You don't laugh."

"What's it to you?"

"Nothing. I'm just saying."

This is why I limit my connection with people. They start to pay attention and ask questions. I look at Peter, the flop of brown hair that falls onto his forehead every time he moves his head. He is not a danger to me now. He's just talking.

"You seem serious today," he says. "Something bothering you?"

My thoughts drift to my last mission, a girl's eyes looking up at me in a silent plea for mercy.

"Have you ever done anything you regret?" I say. The words slip out before I realize what I'm saying.

"That's some question," Peter says.

Peter is sixteen like me. But he is a normal kid from the suburbs, a kid in eleventh grade, a kid who thinks he knows what's going on in the world but who has seen nothing.

I'm sixteen, but I've already lived two lives. I've seen people die. I've done the killing myself.

"Forget I asked," I say.

He doesn't speak, just walks with me through the forest that leads back to camp.

"My brother," he says. "That's what I regret."

"I didn't know you had a brother."

"He doesn't talk to me anymore."

"You had a fight?"

"He was using drugs a couple years ago and I found out and told my parents. Now he's at boarding school on the other side of the country, and I'm the asshole brother who betrayed him."

"If he was using, you might have saved his life."

"Yeah, maybe. Or maybe it was just a phase and I ruined his life. Hard to know."

"I think you did the right thing."

"That's what the counselor at school told me. But I don't know. If I was loyal, maybe I would have kept my mouth shut."

I look at Peter. I detect no lies, no subterfuge. He's not trying to trick me or make me like him. He's just telling a story, as friends do.

"What about you?" Peter says. "What do you regret?"

I asked the question, but I can't answer it. I'm forbidden to give details about missions past or present.

I live a secret life. Nobody knows the things I do or why I do them.

"A girl." That's all I can say.

"A hot girl?"

I smile. "Very hot."

"Did you two sleep together?"

"I don't want to talk about it."

Peter is arm's length away, inside the kill zone.

"I just wonder what you regret about her," he says.

The dinner bell rings for the third time.

"Everything," I say.

My father.

I am twelve years old, the time before The Program changed my life forever. My father is next to me, his arm warm around my shoulders.

When I am awake, I don't think about my father's death. My feelings about it are buried far away, where they cannot distract me. But when I am asleep, the memories return, along with the incredible pain of losing him.

In the dream, my father has something important to tell me. It's something he needs me to understand, something critical to my survival.

I lean toward him. He opens his mouth to speak—

But instead of his voice, I hear a popping noise, something like the sound a can of soda makes when you pull the top.

The noise is familiar to me. It is the pop of a gas grenade, and in my mind's eye, I see the familiar oblong metal encasement, a top with a pull ring. Yank and throw, and the grenade hits the floor and rolls as it has been designed to do.

If this was a real noise, it will be followed by something else.

The hissing sound of escaping gas. That is what I hear now.

Move. Quickly.

By the time I know the grenade is real, my body is already in motion. I roll out of my bunk and hit the floor.

I stay low because gas rises. It's a warm summer's night, but I know from my training that the gas will be warmer than the air at initial release. It will rise until it hits the roof, then collapse on itself and fall toward the floor. I have time. Seconds. Perhaps as much as half a minute.

No more.

I know all this without thinking. I know it instinctually, and that is enough, because I have been trained to act on instinct. Not to weigh the options, do a pros-and-cons list, strategize. There is a time to do all of those things, and then there is a different time.

A time to survive.

I am on my belly in the dark now, moving past the sleeping campers around me, crawling toward the bathroom area in the rear of the cabin.

I listen to the gas releasing. A single canister.

It's a twelve-person cabin. I consider the size of the room, calculate the expansion and absorption rate. I consider the purpose of a gas grenade. There are three primary uses of gas attack:

Cloak.
Disable.
Kill.

Whatever the purpose of this attack, I suspect I am the target.

After my last assignment, I was told to wait somewhere for

further instructions. A certain hotel in a certain city. That is standard operating procedure for my employer, The Program. I carry out a mission, and then I wait for The Program to send me instructions.

But as I sat in an empty hotel room in a strange city, there was nothing but time to think about the things I had done. When the thinking got too loud, I went for a walk. The walk led me to a bus. The bus brought me to Vermont, where an ad posted on a local diner's wall led me to the camp and a CIT position.

I wanted to get away from the mission, the thoughts of the girl, and the dream of my father that comes when I wait.

But the thoughts and dreams followed me. Evidently so did someone else.

I have an idea who it might be, but I can't be sure. With a gas grenade releasing in the cabin, I have no recourse but to protect myself.

Defend first, ask questions later.

I consider all this in the fifteen seconds it takes to inch on my belly toward the bathroom area in the back of the cabin, feel my way up the drainpipe under the sink, and reach across cool porcelain to find someone's hand towel.

I wet the towel and wrap it around my face to make a temporary mask. It should buy me a few extra seconds.

There is a rear exit out of the cabin, but I'm sure it will be guarded.

I pause on the floor of the bathroom and I listen.

No footsteps. That means they are waiting for the gas to do its job.

That's how I would undertake an operation like this. Seal the cabin, slide the gas canister through the front door, and wait. Then I would complete my assignment.

What is *their* assignment right now? I don't intend to be here to find out.

With the wet towel on my face, I make my way, not toward the front or rear door, but to a removable wooden panel in the bathroom floor. My guess is that their recon has not uncovered its existence, because ours is the only cabin that has it. A secret Color Wars project from years past. That's the story I was told, and it's the reason I chose this cabin. I pop open the trapdoor and drop into the cool dirt below.

I do not know what's waiting for me in the darkness outside, so I must be ready for anything.

THERE ARE SOLDIERS HERE.

I make out a handful of them in the dark, an advance team, tactical aiming lasers playing across the wood of the cabin above me.

I roll along the ground, exposed for a few precious seconds until the motion carries me under the frame of a neighboring cabin.

Peter's cabin.

I do not owe him anything. I've only been here for three days. I have stayed nearly invisible, my personality softened, everything about me fuzzed down like a dimmer switch turned to its lowest setting. Only Peter knows me, or at least the me I want him to know.

Maybe he knows more. I've talked more than usual. I've needed to talk.

Still, I should not care about him. Instead I should roll from beneath this cabin to another, hopscotching from cover to cover until I am on the edge of the camp and I can disappear into the woods.

But I cannot let Peter suffer for befriending me. I have to warn him.

So I pull myself from under his cabin, run my fingers up the wooden slats, and find a ledge beneath the window. There is only one soldier nearby, his laser aiming away, so I dead-lift myself up by my fingertips, tilt up the window covering, and peer through the screen.

There is a gas canister here, too, releasing its contents in the center of the floor.

I gasp a lungful of clean air and thrust myself through the window screen. I stay low and move through the darkness, just under the layer of gas.

I quickly locate Peter lying in his bunk.

I shake him. "Wake up!"

He's nonrespondent. I lean down and listen to his chest. His heart's still beating, slow but steady. His breathing is shallow but regular.

The boy next to him is in the same condition. And the one next to him.

Knockout gas. That's what is in these grenades.

I know now that Peter will survive, so I fling myself back through the window to the outside.

The gas is everywhere now.

It rolls from the cabin doors and floats across the ground like fog in the moonlight.

I cannot help Peter. It's too late for that. So I will help myself.

I run.

I fling myself against the side of a cabin, keeping my body close to the wall for cover. I wait for a moment, then I dart out again, moving cabin to cabin toward the safety of the forest that surrounds the camp.

I make it to the farthermost cabin, but before I can make a break for the woods I see a mass of soldiers coming toward me, rising out of the darkness of the forest. There are at least two dozen of them, professional soldiers in tight formation following on the heels of the advance team. They are in Tychem Coveralls with breathers and night-vision goggles. Their guns are up and at the ready, lasers criss-crossing the area as they search for me.

The soldiers are well trained and highly equipped. Could they be working for The Program? The Program doesn't have military assets in the formal sense, but their reach is enormous, their resources nearly unlimited.

But if it's not The Program, who else could it be? I think about the many other groups I've brushed up against in previous missions. Rogue elements of the Mossad, Ministry of State Security agents from China, SZRU operatives from the Ukraine. None of them are likely to be able to track me, much less to the woods of Vermont, but now is not the time to take chances.

I must escape.

If I step away from the cover of the cabin wall, my heat signa-ture will give me away. My only hope is to stay where the gas is heaviest. It may disrupt their enhanced vision long enough for me to get away.

I dive for the nearest cloud of gas, but the soldiers are on me before I can do anything, a closing maneuver that overwhelms with sheer force.

I freeze, caught in the open.

The laser sights of their weapons play over my body. They sur-round me, circling, two dozen men with guns, with technological advantage, with overwhelming power.

I rapid-scan the area, looking for angles, routes of escape, any way to reduce their firing solutions, but I do not find any.

I am caught.

I note the feet of the soldiers around me shuffling back and forth. Nerves. Overwhelming numbers and power, yet they are nervous.

Which means they know who I am.

How is that possible?

Suddenly the circle parts, two of the soldiers stepping back to make space. A man comes out of the shadows and strides purposefully into the circle. He wears no protective suit, carries no weapons. Even before I see his face, I know who he is. I know from the certainty with which he moves. I have not seen him in more than two years, but we have spoken on the phone dozens of times as he guides me through my assignments.

This is the man who trained me.

The man I call Father.

He is not my real father. He is something else. My commander.

Now I know who has come for me. It is The Program. But why have they come like this, with dozens of soldiers?

I watch Father's face. It is impassive, unreadable.

Something contracts in my chest, my breathing suddenly shallow.

I give the feeling a name:

Fear.